The Diary

THE
DIARY

EILEEN GOUDGE

Vanguard Press
A Member of the Perseus Books Group

Copyright © 2009 by Eileen Goudge

Published by Vanguard Press
A Member of the Perseus Books Group

Set in 12.5 point Centaur by the Perseus Books Group

Vanguard Press books are available at special discounts for
bulk purchases in the U.S. by corporations, institutions, and
other organizations. For more information, please contact the
Special Markets Department at the Perseus Books Group,
2300 Chestnut Street, Suite 200, Philadelphia, PA 19103,
or call (800) 810-4145, ext. 5000, or e-mail
special.markets@perseusbooks.com.

Library of Congress Cataloging-in-Publication Data
Goudge, Eileen.
  The diary / Eileen Goudge.
    p. cm.
  ISBN 978-1-59315-543-8 (hardcover : alk. paper) — ISBN
978-1-59315-529-2 (pbk. : alk. paper) I. Mothers—
Diaries—Fiction. 2. Mothers and daughters—Fiction.
3. Domestic fiction. I. Title.
  PS3557.O838D53 2009
  813'.54—dc22
                                        2008051569

10 9 8 7 6 5 4 3 2 1

For my parents, Jim and Mary Goudge,

who never stopped holding hands

The life of every man is a diary in which
he means to write one story,
and writes another . . .

—JAMES M. BARRIE

AUTHOR'S NOTE

This novel was inspired by a true story from my parents'
lives. The details shall remain under wraps so as not to
spoil the ending. Here's what I can tell you: My father
served in World War II. He and my mother met shortly after the war. She spotted him at a dance hall called the Co-
conut Grove and told her brother-in-law to go over and
introduce himself—and, by the way, to be sure to mention
that he had an attractive sister-in-law. My father took the
bait, and they danced all night, by their own account. They
went on to marry and have six children.

Before we came along, my father made a living doing
caricatures at county fairs. He earned enough that way to
make a down payment on their first home. But the realities
of supporting such a large brood eventually forced him to
take a more mundane route: After a brief stint selling
Fuller brushes door to door, he became an insurance agent
for State Farm. His creative side was fulfilled by buying

and renovating old houses, which he turned into rental properties.

Their love story didn't become fully known to me and my siblings until later in our lives. We saw them only as Mom and Dad. My mom took care of the house and baked her own bread. My father arrived home from work each day carrying a briefcase. Through a secret cache of old photos and stories from friends and relatives, and even a few selected ones from my mother as she grew older and felt we could handle some of the less sanitized aspects of their marriage, we learned more about them as real people: their hopes and dreams, their disappointments, and most of all their undying passion for each other. When my father passed away, my mother told us she wasn't going to mourn him because she knew she would be joining him before long. Ten years later, she did just that. Today they're buried side by side in a cemetery in the seaside town they called home.

The story of Elizabeth and AJ is dedicated to my parents.

CHAPTER ONE

The diary was bound in maroon leather dulled with age, its gilt tooling worn away in spots. Sewn into the binding was a satin bookmarker, once red, now faded to the ashy pink of a dried, pressed rose. The diary seemed to carry the scent of dried roses as well, the merest hint, like the long-forgotten bundles of sachet the two daughters had been finding tucked in the backs of drawers throughout the house all this past week.

As Emily withdrew it from the cardboard carton she'd been rooting through, the small key inserted in its metal clasp fell to the dusty floorboards with a soft plink, disappearing into the gloaming of an attic crammed to the rafters and lit only by the errant rays of sunlight that had managed to slip in under the eaves. The clasp gave easily when she pried at it with her thumbnail, the worn cover falling back with a creak of arthritic spine to reveal an entry penned in handwriting so neatly rounded and girlish, it was a moment before she recognized it as their mother's.

She idly remarked to her sister, "I didn't know Mom kept a diary."

"A diary? Hmmm," Sarah murmured distractedly. She was kneeling on the floor beside Emily, her rear end resting on her sneakered heels, absorbed in sorting through another carton filled with odds and ends. "God, can you believe all this stuff? She must've saved every single card and letter, not to mention all our school report cards." She plucked one from a crumpled manila envelope marked "Sarah." "Oh, Lord. There's that D-plus I got in Mr. Grimaldi's class. All As and Bs except that one stupid D. Remember how mad Mom was? Not at me but at my teacher. She marched straight down there and told him that if a smart girl like me had practically flunked his class, it was because he didn't know how to teach. I was so embarrassed!" She smiled at the memory, eyes gleaming with unshed tears.

"How could I forget?" It hadn't been just that one incident. Their mother had been a tigress when it came to her children, questioning and sometimes berating anyone who dared criticize them when she viewed the criticism as unjust; making sure they got the best education; gently nudging Emily, the shier of the two, into the forefront whenever she appeared in danger of being overshadowed by her more outgoing sister. For Elizabeth, husband and children had always come first.

"I wonder if the old man ever recovered," said Sarah, chuckling softly as she shook her head.

Emily's attention was drawn back to the diary, which had fallen open to about the midway point. She struggled to make out their mother's neat schoolgirl's handwriting in the dim light. Her pulse quickened as a passage jumped out at her. She called urgently to her sister, "Sarah, come quick. You have to see this!"

Sarah crab-walked over to have a look, pushing a scrap of blond hair behind one ear as she leaned to peer over Emily's shoulder. After a moment, she exclaimed softly, "Wow. Looks like this diary wasn't the only secret she kept." She looked up at her sister, her eyes wide and her normally animated face slack with puzzlement. "What do you make of it?"

Sarah was the rounder of the two, anchored to the earth in a way that made her seem sensible and dependable, which she was. Emily, the more excitable one, was built like a rocket poised for lift-off. Sarah had their father's fair hair and blue eyes, while Emily favored their mother: tall and slim-hipped, with dark hair that grew to a widow's peak on her forehead like the point on one of the heart-shaped construction-paper cutouts she'd been unearthing from cardboard cartons all day—various Valentine's Day projects made by her and her sister through the years.

Emily shook her head, equally bewildered. Then a new, troubling thought occurred to her. "Do you think Dad knew?"

Their father had passed away the year before. His ashes were in an urn on the fireplace mantel downstairs, where their mother had been keeping them while purportedly trying to decide where they ought to be scattered.

"Maybe it was before they were a couple," said Sarah.

"No. Look at the date." Emily flipped back to the first entry, where the date was clearly marked: *July 3, 1951.*

"The year she married Dad." Sarah's voice emerged as a cracked whisper.

Their mother had been twenty-one when she and Bob Marshall had wed in December of 1951, just before he'd shipped out to Korea. Sarah had been born five years later, Emily three years after that.

Emily, seated cross-legged on the floor, stared sightlessly at the jumbled pile she'd unearthed from her box: an old clock missing one of its hands, a manila envelope stuffed full of yellowing receipts, back issues of magazines, tattered paperbacks, a JFK campaign button, and an old sombrero with a hole in its brim—a souvenir from a family trip to Acapulco. "You know how she was always telling us Dad was the only man she ever loved?" she mused aloud before bringing her head sharply round to face Sarah. "Do you think that's just what she *wanted* us to believe?"

The two sisters sat in silence for a moment.

Finally Sarah replied staunchly, "No. She loved him."

Emily nodded thoughtfully. No one who'd ever seen their parents together could have doubted that. Still . . . "According to this, he wasn't the *only* man she loved." She peered at the diary, frowning.

"If that's the case, it must've been before she and Dad were serious about each other." Sarah found it impossible to envision their churchgoing, pie-baking, S&H Green Stamp–collecting mother involved in something as tawdry as sneaking around behind their father's back, even if it had been before they were married.

"No. Look." Emily brought her sister's attention back to the first entry, where their mother had written that she was expecting a proposal from Bob soon—proof that they'd been deeply involved at the time. Then Emily flipped to the earlier passage she'd bookmarked, dated August 12, 1951, just five weeks later.

"I don't see how it's possible for a human heart to hold all that I feel for AJ. Can a heart burst from too much love? How can it be that Bob hasn't noticed? Whenever I'm with him, I'm sure it's written all over my face."

Sarah shook her head slowly, still struggling to digest it. "What I want to know is who is this AJ character? How come we never heard of him before?" she demanded huffily.

They both knew the answer. Who had there been to tell such tales? Both Bob and Bets had been only children, so there were no aunts or uncles to fill the girls in on family lore. Their parents hadn't been much for telling stories about the past, either. Now Emily thought she understood why: When keeping secrets, it was best to keep the past tucked away.

"I don't know, but I intend to find out." Emily rose with a decisive upward thrust, clutching the diary in one hand.

Sarah struggled to her feet with a bit more difficulty, wincing as her cramped joints popped in release. The days when she'd been head cheerleader in high school seemed distant from the vantage point of her forty-nine years, with the twenty pounds she'd packed onto her small frame with each of her boys. Despite her best efforts, she'd been unable to shed the extra weight.

"Maybe we should wait until we can ask Mom," she said, placing a hand on Emily's arm.

"You're kidding, right?" Emily gave her an incredulous look. "You know what the doctor said. We shouldn't expect a miracle."

"Still . . . " Sarah remained troubled.

It was true that their mother's prognosis wasn't encouraging—six months earlier she'd suffered a massive stroke that had left her unable to speak or move, even to feed herself. But Sarah, and to a lesser degree Emily, continued to hold out hope nonetheless. At her bedside, they searched for glimmers of the woman they'd known, just as, when they were children, they'd once searched in vain for arrowheads in the vacant lot behind their house. Meanwhile, the white-haired old lady with the blank eyes and frozen rictus of a mouth who'd once been the vibrant, outspoken Elizabeth Marshall remained suspended in this twilight state, tended to around the clock by the nurses at the Miriam Hastings McDonald extended care facility. The sisters took turns visiting her there, the facility being conveniently located midway between Sarah, who lived with her husband and two sons, and Emily, with her three cats and newly issued divorce decree.

Some of Emily's resolution fled. As she stood in the close atmosphere of the attic, motes of dust dancing in a beam of sunlight angling across the floor at her feet, she felt small and lost. Her narrow shoulders sagged with the weight of all the decisions she and her sister had had to make in a short span of time: where to place their mother after her release from the hospital, whether or not to sell her house—the pink, gabled Victorian they'd grown up in—and what sort of advance funeral arrangements were to be made. Their mother had been the soul of organization in most respects, but about that she'd been maddeningly vague. Whenever one of them would broach the topic, she'd smile and say, "You girls will know what to do when the time comes."

"I know. I hate it, too." Emily sighed. In some ways, it was as though their mother were already gone—all that was left a body of no use to her or anyone, an empty shell washed ashore by the tide. "But I can't just sit on this. I have to know."

Sarah looked unconvinced, and Emily thought she understood why: Reading other people's diaries was what you did after they were dead.

There was also the matter of their father not having been their mother's one and only. This was what Emily found most troubling. Their dad hadn't been one to wear his emotions on his sleeve—a reserve their mother had chalked up to psychological scars sustained in combat—but she didn't doubt that he'd loved them. Emily was certain that after their marriage, he'd never even looked at a woman other than his wife. This was the same man, after all, who'd been deacon of their church, past president of his Masonic Lodge, and a dedicated employee of the same firm for more than forty years. The term "one-woman man" had been invented for Bob Marshall, and for him, that woman had been Elizabeth. How awful, Emily thought, to find out that theirs hadn't been the storybook romance she'd always thought was a given!

But her desire to know the truth was greater than any fear that she'd be opening a Pandora's Box. Her sister, she could see, was leaning in that direction as well. Sarah had a habit of tugging on her lower lip when in the throes of making a decision, and right now it was pulled down so far that Emily could see the bridge where she'd lost a tooth after being hit by a runaway croquet ball as a teenager.

Finally Sarah came to a decision. "All right. I'll phone Jeff and tell him not to wait on me for supper."

"While you do that, I'll go see if there's still some of that wine left in the fridge," said Emily as she headed for the stairs, the diary clutched firmly to her breast. "I have a feeling we're going to need it."

CHAPTER TWO

Dear Diary,

Bob asked me to marry him today. Well, he didn't come right out and ask. That's not his style. He asked what I wanted for my birthday in September, and I told him to surprise me. So he says, with this little twinkle in his eye, "Oh, I already have something picked out. I just hope it's what you want." When I asked for a hint, he said, "All I can tell you is that it comes in a small box." Now, what could that mean other than what I think it means? And wouldn't that be just like Bob, wanting it to be a surprise but not wanting to take any chances, either? As if there could be any doubt, given that we've been together almost four years. Besides, everyone has been talking about it for so long, it feels like we're already engaged. I wouldn't be surprised to find out that Mother has been secretly planning the wedding this whole time.

But nothing's been settled just yet. I have the whole rest of the summer to be Elizabeth Harvey, single girl extraordinaire. Who knows? I may just decide to run away and join the circus. Can't you see me as a trapeze artist, swinging through the air in my itty-bitty costume? Wouldn't Mother have a fit? Which reminds me, the county fair is tomorrow. Afterward there's to be the usual picnic and fireworks. Bob and I are riding over with Mother in her car. At last year's fair, Gunther Willis's prize Brahman bull escaped from its pen and caused quite the ruckus when it tried to mount Missy Carruther's pony. I wonder what excitement is in store this year.

∽

"Go on. Don't be shy."

Elizabeth Harvey cast an imperious eye on the young man who was now motioning for her to have a seat. AJ sat perched on a stool before an easel on which a large sketch pad was propped, surrounded by other artisans hawking their wares—weavers, potters, wood-carvers, and the like. Displayed on another easel beside him was a caricature in pastels of a freckle-faced little girl—quite a skilled one, she noted. He was smiling up at her, knees spread in a pose as impudent as his pitch, fair hair luffing in the welcome breeze that blew through the fairgrounds, carrying the smell of hot dogs and kettle corn and the more fecund waft from the 4-H barn. His fingers were rainbow-hued from the pastels scattered over the easel's tray. His eyes, the color of the faded blue jeans he wore, seemed to mock her in some way.

"I'm not here to get my picture drawn. I only stopped to say hello," she informed him, all at once regretting the impulse that had made her pause at the sight of a familiar face in this unfamiliar setting.

Undeterred, he asked, "What's your hurry?"

"I have to—" She started to reply that she was on her way to the main pavilion to meet her boyfriend, but AJ didn't let her finish.

"Think of it as a souvenir," he went on in the same cocky vein. "One day when you look back on this, you'll remember it as the county fair where you had your carica-ture done by your old pal AJ."

Her cheeks warmed at the seemingly ironic reference to their childhood friendship, and she felt a twinge of guilt for having allowed that friendship to fade—though was she really to blame? He was the one, after all, who'd spurned every overture since then. And after the incident in high school that had resulted in his being sent away, he'd dropped out of her life altogether. This was the first time she'd seen him in more than three years. "I suppose this is what you call making an honest living?" She in-jected just the right note of playfulness into her voice so he wouldn't take offense but at the same time would know that she didn't think making eyes at young women and having them pay for the privilege fell into the category of an honest living. Even if he was someone she'd known since kindergarten.

His shoulders rolled in an indolent shrug. "Beats cut-ting hay."

He had a point. This time of year, nearly every able-bodied man in the county who didn't have a crop of his own to bring in was recruited to work in the neighboring fields. She took a mincing step in his direction, one hand on her straw hat to keep it anchored in place, though the breeze was a mild one, just enough to flutter its ribbons. "How much are you charging?" she inquired.

"Five bucks a pop."

"Isn't that kind of steep?"

He flashed her a lazy grin, somehow all the more appealing because of a crooked eyetooth that had never benefited from orthodontia. Under the snugly fitting white T-shirt he wore with his jeans, the muscles in his arms and chest were clearly defined. He reminded her of a mountain lion, lithe and sinewy and built for speed; he seemed coiled to spring even while sitting perfectly still. "You can always frame it and hang it on your wall," he told her. "Can't put a price on that."

"You seem to have a high opinion of your artistic talent," she observed coolly.

"Oh, I wouldn't say that," he demurred with what she might have deemed modesty if she hadn't known him to be proud to the point of arrogance. "It's just a little parlor trick I picked up along the way."

A reminder that while she was going to football games and dances, he was spending the second semester of their senior year at the Silas Kingston Youth Detention Facility in Riverton. AJ, for reasons known only to him, had set his uncle's car on fire. The act had sent shock waves through their small community and catapulted him overnight from an aloof and somewhat disreputable figure on the fringes of the sock-hop/pep-rally world Elizabeth inhabited to the most-talked-about kid in school. Yet despite all the talk, nobody seemed to have a handle on AJ. Although gossip swirled around him, mostly having to do with girls with whom he was rumored to have had his way, he was a mystery even to classmates who'd known him as long as she had.

Elizabeth knew him better than most, she supposed. They'd been playmates as children. He'd been just another kid back then, if a bit more free-spirited than most. But the tragedy that left him orphaned at the age of nine altered him in other ways. After he went to live with his grandparents, he became withdrawn to the point of being antisocial. His only friends, if you could call them that, were class troublemakers Gunnar Nielson and Del Hannigan. With Elizabeth, who'd once ridden on the back of his bike and with whom he'd shared Orange Crushes and played kick-the-can, he grew more and more distant with each passing year. In class he seldom acknowledged her presence, and if their eyes happened to meet when they passed each other in the halls, he never greeted her with anything more than a half-cocked smile or ironic arch of the brow. During their junior year, when they were briefly thrown together as lab partners in biology, she made an attempt to rekindle their old friendship, but it was met with a coolness that bordered on disdain. Convinced that he found her silly and frivolous, not worthy of his time or attention, she decided he wasn't worthy of hers, either. Still, she remained curious about him, and at times that curiosity drove her to distraction. Why, she wondered, was he the only boy immune to her charms? She'd see him with other girls not half as pretty as she and feel oddly rejected. Then she'd tell herself it was silly to feel that way when she already had a boyfriend—one who was sweet and caring—and she had no romantic interest in AJ in any event.

It was the same curiosity that kept her rooted to the spot now, any thoughts of the boyfriend she'd been on her way to meet far from her mind. "Are you any good at it?" she asked, edging a step closer.

AJ cocked his head, studying her with a keen, professional eye. The canvas tarp shielding him from the sun was torn in spots, and with each new gust of wind, little wavelets of sunlight found their way through the rips to shimmy over his face. Not an especially handsome face, she thought, but certainly an arresting one: narrow and sharp-featured as if honed by hard, clean strokes of an ax, with high, planed cheekbones and tanned skin the dusky gold of just-pressed cider. His heavy brows, the color of the charcoal pencil his fingers were loosely curled about, stood out in marked contrast to his fair hair. His eyes were so blue they seemed to crackle.

"Tell you what," he said. "Let me have a go at you, and if you don't like it, it's on the house."

Elizabeth felt herself prickle with unaccustomed heat. She was glad her mother wasn't here, for she would have railed at the mere thought of any boy "having a go" at her daughter, however innocent his intentions. (Mildred Harvey was at that moment sequestered in the main pavilion with the panel judging pickles and preserves, a job she took as seriously as a high government office.) The fact that it was "the Keener boy"—as AJ had been known ever since his parents had died in that auto wreck and he'd gone to live with his mother's folks, Joe and Sally Keener— would have rendered her positively apoplectic.

For her part, Elizabeth wouldn't have minded if he *had* made a pass. Oh, she'd have made a show of minding, but only because it was expected. Among her kind, the only acceptable response to such crude behavior (not that any man in Emory would've dared make a pass at the daughter of Mildred Harvey) was to either turn a blind eye or fell the would-be Lothario with a withering glance. Should the fellow persist, a sharp scolding, or in extreme instances a slap across the face, might be in order. That a good girl might fall prey to such a seduction was unthinkable. Elizabeth, at twenty, was educated in the ways of the birds and the bees—it was the modern age, after all—but for unmarried ladies of her class, the region of the female anatomy discreetly referred to as the "flower of womanhood" was strictly off-limits to members of the opposite sex and even, for the most part—aside from basic hygiene—to oneself. There had been some progress since the corseted era of her mother's youth, but for a young lady to be known as "easy," even in the year 1951, was about as ruinous as having a reputation for setting cars on fire.

But while Elizabeth had her standards, she often wondered what it would be like. She'd only gone so far as to let Bob remove her blouse and, once, her bra (they were practically engaged, which made it permissible) while they'd been steaming up the windows of his Buick coupe. She wouldn't have described it as unexciting, but there hadn't been any of the unexpurgated thrills of *Lady Chatterley's Lover*, a contraband copy of which had recently fallen into her hands via her friend Dot, who'd obtained it from a cousin in England. Elizabeth had breathlessly devoured the novel in a single night behind the locked door of her bedroom, yet whenever she tried to imagine herself in similar throes of passion with Bob, it struck her as a bit silly.

However much she looked forward to their wedding day, she could never quite envision him weaving wildflowers through her pubic hair or assigning nicknames to their private parts.

Now, squirming a bit under AJ's scrutiny, she thought, *I bet nothing would embarrass him.* The thought sent a fresh surge of blood to her cheeks. If her hat hadn't been partially hiding her face, it would have been apparent to anyone looking on that AJ was having a decidedly bracing effect on her. But, amazingly, even that wasn't enough to make her walk away.

"All right, it's a deal," she told him. "Just don't make me look bad, that's all I ask."

Another man might have insisted that no artist could possibly make her look bad. Elizabeth was well aware that she was exceptionally pretty. Even if she hadn't known it from looking in the mirror, the steady flow of compliments she'd been receiving all her life would have confirmed it. When she'd been a baby in her carriage, it had been common, according to Mildred, for people to stop on the street to admire her. Nowadays, with her dark hair and classic features, her slim hips and shapely bosom, she frequently drew comparisons to her namesake, Elizabeth Taylor. The only difference between her and the star of *National Velvet,* it was often said, was that Elizabeth Harvey's eyes were hazel instead of violet, the color of greenstone shot through with veins of ore.

But if AJ found her attractive, he didn't remark on it. "Have a seat," he said, motioning once more toward the wooden folding chair opposite his easel. She gingerly lowered herself into it, glancing nervously about as she did. But though there were people milling about, on their way to the food stalls or the dime-toss or the Tilt-a-Whirl grinding away to its tinkling refrain, she saw no one she recognized who would be likely to report back to her mother. The fairgrounds were located in the neighboring township of Shaw Creek, twenty miles east of Emory, and thus drew crowds from two counties. It wasn't difficult to get lost in the crowd.

AJ squinted slightly as if to set her in his sights, then began to sketch with quick, sure strokes. Observing him out of the corner of her eye as she held her pose, Elizabeth was surprised and impressed. Had he been this good at drawing in school? If so, he'd kept it under wraps because she couldn't recall having seen a single piece of artwork. In those days, when he wasn't prowling the halls like a lone wolf, he sat in class without contributing much. (Despite which, his grades never seemed to suffer—another mystery about AJ.) She found herself remembering other things as well, like how she occasionally used to catch him eyeing her and her friends, wearing an expression of bemused disdain as if he found the whole scene, with its pom-poms and letter jackets and class rings, vaguely pathetic. Which was odd, she reflected, since most people would have thought it was AJ's life that was pathetic.

From the age of nine he'd lived with his grandparents just outside town, along one of the county roads in an area called Cement Town, so dubbed because of the cement factory that dominated the landscape. Unfortunately, jobs weren't the only thing the factory provided: Its belching

stacks deposited a gritty dust, like a gray pall, over everything within a one-mile radius. It was said by those who
lived in Cement Town that no amount of hosing or sweeping could remove that dust. It was embedded in the weave
of carpets and curtains and upholstery. It clung to shelves,
and to the books and knickknacks that lined those shelves.
It ran like a line drawn in gray chalk along baseboards and
ceiling moldings. It worked its way into hair and clothing
and the treads of shoes. At times it could even be felt grit-
ting like graphite between one's back teeth.

Dead center in all that grayness sat Joe and Sally
Keener's small grocery store. How they eked out a living
was anyone's guess, given the modest means of their customers. Everyone, including the Keeners themselves, must
have wondered how they managed to stay afloat year after
year, peddling jarred and boxed goods with more dust on
them than on the pavement outside, shrunken heads of let-
tuce, gray-tinted lunch meats of indeterminate origin, and
crackers and loaves of bread long past their expiration
dates. The likeliest reason was that they were the only gro-
cers for miles around and many of the people who lived in
Cement Town didn't own cars.

Once, on her way to visit a friend at one of the outlying
farms, she stopped at the Keeners' store, where AJ worked
after school and on weekends. She wasn't quite sure what
prompted her to do so, other than vague curiosity about
AJ's life outside school, but when she encountered him
stocking shelves in back, the blank look he gave her was
enough to drive away any warm words of greeting she'd

been about to utter. Flustered, she muttered a quick hello and asked if they had any Dr. Pepper.

He shook his head, replying, just shy of rudely, "Just Coke and Pepsi," before getting back to work.

She went away feeling rebuffed, though she told herself there was no reason it should matter one way or the other what AJ thought of her. After all, it wasn't as though she cared about *him*.

Nonetheless, she puzzled over the mystery of the boy who appeared entirely self-contained in a world that crowded him on all sides and who was proud in a way that bore no relation either to his station in life or his achievements. A pride that certainly didn't derive from being the apple of his grandparents' eye: Joe and Sally Keener weren't the warmest of people, and their attitude toward their grandson, the few times Elizabeth had seen them at school functions, was one of grim duty. She could see them now in her mind's eye: two absolutely colorless people, as stark and gray as everything else in Cement Town.

She was struck by the marked contrast with AJ. It was as if God had determined that all the life leached from Joe and Sally Keener should go to their grandson. Even the air around him seemed charged. Watching him was like watching a blade held to a grindstone as it whirred; she could almost see the sparks shooting off him.

At last he tore the finished caricature from his pad, extending it toward her without comment.

She gazed at it with interest that quickly gave way to dismay. It wasn't an exact likeness, nor was it meant to be, but he'd captured her to a T: a large cartoon head dominated by sultry eyes and pouty lips, capped by an old-fashioned bonnet, which sat atop a miniature cartoon body in a hoop skirt and ruffled pantaloons. In one hand was a staff, like Little Bo Peep's. In place of sheep, a herd of love-struck swains trailed after her.

"Is that really how you see me?" she managed to choke out.

AJ shrugged, tossing a stub of pastel into the box of supplies at his feet. "The trick is to sketch the first thing that comes to mind," he told her. "That's what I thought of when I was drawing you."

"That I'm a tease?" She rose to her feet, glaring at him. "For your information, I've had the same boyfriend for the past four years!"

AJ smiled flatly, and some unreadable emotion flickered in the depths of his blue-denim eyes. "Yeah, I know. I ran into Bob the other day. He mentioned that you two were still an item. Congratulations." He made it sound as though it were a bull-riding event in a rodeo and he was congratulating her for having stayed in the saddle longer than any of her competitors.

Annoyed, she blurted, "We're going to be married."

Elizabeth regretted the words as soon as they were out. What on earth had possessed her to say that? Bob hadn't even asked her yet. Though it was generally considered a foregone conclusion, it would be highly embarrassing should word get out about their "engagement" before he actually popped the question. And if for some reason Bob didn't propose? She would never live it down.

"I'd appreciate it if you didn't mention it to anyone," she added, her cheeks warming. "We're keeping it a secret for the time being."

AJ shot her a puzzled look, as if he found the need for secrecy a bit odd, given the fact that she and Bob had been going together practically forever. But his only comment, delivered in his patented arch tone that verged on condescending, was, "Don't tell me you're planning to elope?"

"No, of course not. It's just . . . it's complicated." The fire in her cheeks spread to engulf her entire face. Nervously she toyed with the top button of her blouse, where a pulse throbbed at the base of her throat, her gaze fixed on AJ's muscular forearms streaked with Easter-egg-colored dust.

"Really? I would have thought just the opposite."

She bristled. "Are you saying I'm predictable?"

"No. Just that I'm sure you two will be very happy together." Again that half-mocking tone.

"Thank you," she said stiffly. "Now, I'm afraid I must be going." She handed back the drawing and dug into her handbag, extracting a five-dollar bill from her wallet.

But AJ refused her money. "It's on me," he said. "A deal's a deal."

"I never said it wasn't good," she allowed grudgingly. "It's just . . . well, it's not very flattering is all." Hearing the words come out of her mouth, she felt that his opinion of her was justified.

He smiled. "Caricatures aren't supposed to be flattering. That's actually the point."

"All right. I get it." She glowered at him, tucking the money back into her wallet. *To hell with him,* she thought.

There was no rule that said you had to pay someone to insult you.

AJ took hold of her arm as she was turning to go. "No, I don't think you do," he said in a low voice that shocked her—it was that of someone bound to her by something far more intimate than any of the exchanges they'd had thus far. "But if you'd care to stick around, I'd be happy to explain."

Elizabeth knew, she absolutely *knew*, that there was no possible reason for her to stay and listen to his explanation. But somehow she remained rooted to the spot. There was something about AJ that was making her act in ways contrary to her nature, and she didn't like it one bit. Why did she even care what he thought of her? Soon she'd be married to a man who thought the sun rose and set with her.

Despite all that, she found herself rearing back, hands on hips, to reply, "All right, but this better be good."

AJ didn't know what had possessed him. It wasn't as if he'd set out to insult Elizabeth. And he certainly hadn't intended for it to lead to a confession. But damn if the woman didn't have that effect on him. Wasn't that what had gotten him into trouble in the first place?

"Not here," he said. "Can we go somewhere?"

She hesitated just long enough for him to get the message that she wasn't too keen on the idea before answering, "All right, but I don't have much time. I'm supposed to meet someone." Her boyfriend, no doubt. Fiancé, rather, he corrected himself. The unspoken word was like a piece of gristle lodged between his back teeth.

"It won't take long. Come on, this way," he said, beckoning to her as he turned on his heel.

He didn't bother to pack up his easel and supplies, knowing they wouldn't be disturbed. Nor was he concerned with any potential loss of business. He'd made fifty dollars so far today, with the rest of the long weekend still ahead of him, so he was in good shape. And next week was the county fair in Seneca, and after that the one in Tilden.

He'd been working the circuit for the past two years or so, traveling from one county fair to the next, living out of the beat-up old Studebaker that had become his home and occasionally his bed on those nights when he couldn't afford to spring for a boardinghouse or motel. He made good money, but the work was seasonal. The rest of the year he relied on his savings and the odd jobs he picked up here and there. It was enough to get by.

This was his second summer doing the Shaw Creek fair. But he had yet to take the short trip down the road to Emory to see his grandparents. It wasn't that he hadn't forgiven them—he'd become inured to their coldness long before they'd turned him in for a crime that, in his view, had been nothing more than a case of delayed justice—but he didn't think it likely that they'd forgiven him. They still held him responsible, he suspected, for the unfathomable loss that had delivered him into their care. Not that he'd had anything to do with his mother's death; he hadn't even been with his parents at the time. But logic seldom played a part in the hardening of hearts. The simple fact was that he was alive and she wasn't. For Joe and Sally, there was no getting around that.

He'd had no further run-ins with his uncle, although he'd heard that Cole was gunning for him, that he planned to take a tire iron to AJ's car in retaliation for AJ's having torched his. AJ gave little credence to the rumor. Like most bullies, Cole was a coward at heart—he wouldn't risk picking a fight with someone his own size. He was more interested in getting drunk than in getting even. Recently AJ had read in the paper that his uncle had spent a night in jail on a drunk-driving charge, which meant he must have been royally plastered; usually the sheriff let offenders off with a slap on the wrist. The only thing that surprised AJ was that it hadn't happened sooner.

In all honesty, AJ wouldn't have spared half a brain cell's worth of worry over his uncle if it hadn't been for Elizabeth Harvey. Seeing her today had stirred up all those old feelings again. And now he knew there would be no peace for him until he'd gotten it off his chest.

He skirted the fairgrounds, finding the footpath at the southernmost end, where the beaten earth gave way to a pasture carpeted in knee-high timothy grass. On the other side of the pasture lay the creek where, last summer, he'd cooled off with a dip at the end of each day's work. Some instinct led him in that direction now. He hadn't intended to take her this far—farther than he knew she wanted to go—and each time he glanced back over his shoulder, he was a bit surprised to find her gamely trudging along behind him. She still looked a little ticked off, but mostly puzzled and maybe a bit intrigued. Beautiful women, he knew, had little experience with men who kept them guessing, so she had to be curious as to where all this was leading.

When they finally reached the creek, he was surprised to see how high it was—no doubt a result of the previous week's wet spell. This time last year, he'd been able to wade across to the opposite bank without getting his rolled-up pant legs wet. Now water tumbled over rocks with a sound like pouring rain, gnawing greedily at the banks where they hadn't already been devoured. More faintly came the sounds of children splashing and calling out to each other from the swimming hole upstream. Near it, he recalled, was the shallow cove, hemmed in by rocks and tree roots, where last year at this time he'd stumbled across the stash of watermelons being kept cool for the fair's annual barbe-cue and fireworks display. He could see them in his mind's eye, bobbing like so many legless turtles, and remembered how sweet the one he'd snitched had tasted.

He found a shady spot under a weeping willow where they would be shielded from view. Elizabeth glanced at him skeptically before carefully lowering herself to the ground, tucking her full skirt under her as she did. The skirt was gold with a pattern of red cherries. It made him think of a dress she'd worn often in the fourth grade, a yel-low checked smock that tied in back, with strawberries em-broidered on its crisp white bodice. Back then, whenever he closed his eyes at night, it was those strawberries he saw as he drifted off to sleep.

But if she had any misgivings about following him here, she seemed to have set them aside for the time being.

"What a lovely spot!" she remarked, gazing out at the water chasing itself over the rocks. She stretched her legs out in front of her, smoothing her skirt over her knees.

"Last summer, this was where I came every day to cool off," he told her.

She nodded, seeming all at once awkward in his presence, as though they'd only just met. Which, in a way, was true: This was the most they'd interacted in the fifteen years he'd known her.

"It must get awfully hot, sitting outside all day long," she said.

"You don't notice it so much when you're concentrating on what you're doing."

She turned to eye him curiously. "Funny. I don't recall you being much of an artist in school."

"That's because I never showed my stuff to anyone." He gave a small, pained smile. "It wasn't until my grandma happened to come across my sketch pad one day that she knew what I'd been doing all those hours holed up in my room. That's when my grandparents decided I had too much time on my hands and put me to work in the store. I didn't pick it up again until I was at Silas. They had us do crafts there—occupational therapy, they called it." He paused briefly to register the effect of his words, the way Elizabeth started slightly at his mention of his time in juvenile detention before she quickly rearranged her features into a neutral mask. "I used to kill time doing caricatures of the other guys. I got to be pretty good at it after a while."

"Good at making fun of other people," she said in the huffy tone she'd used earlier.

"Only the thin-skinned ones saw it that way."

"Oh, so now you're saying I'm thin-skinned?" She still sounded mad, but he saw the twinkle in her eye under her raised brow.

"No," he said. "I admit you have a point. I took a cheap shot, and I'm sorry for that."

He hadn't meant to hurt her feelings. Seeing her again, it had all come bubbling up. It was as though his hand had taken on a life of its own while sketching her. It hadn't helped, either, that she was more beautiful than the last time he'd seen her, if such a thing were possible. He'd left behind the memory of a pretty girl and returned to find a woman so lovely it broke his heart just to look at her. Like right now, the way the light reflecting off the water shimmered on her face, accentuating the curve of a cheekbone and painting the tips of her eyelashes gold, showing the down on her cheek that was normally invisible. Her eyes were the green of the water swirling amid the rocks, and the emotions they stirred in him were just as turbulent. It was all he could do to maintain a polite distance when he ached to take her in his arms.

"It would help if I had an explanation." She leveled her gaze at him, arms crossed over her chest.

"All right. I owe you that much, I suppose." He aimed for a lighthearted tone, though the muscles in his chest were tight from holding his emotions in check. It was an effort just to breathe. He hadn't expected it to be so hard after all this time; he'd thought he'd put it all behind him. He stared down at the ground, plucking at a blade of grass as he began the painful process of dredging up the past.

"Do you remember that day you stopped by the store?" However long ago, the memory was etched in his mind. Clearly Elizabeth hadn't forgotten either.

"How could I not? You practically ignored me."

He sighed, feeling as though he were standing at the brink of a gulf that he must now attempt to bridge. "If it seemed like I was ignoring you, it was only because I . . . " He paused, frowning in thought, before summoning the word. "Poleaxed. That's what I was, poleaxed. I couldn't think what you were doing there, in my grandparents' store of all places. My next thought, crazy as it might sound, was that you'd come to see me. It would have been the happiest day of my life if that had been the case. But then you—"

"I asked if you had any Dr. Pepper."

He looked up to find her staring at him with wide eyes.

"That's right," he said, nodding slowly at this new revelation: She didn't just recall the incident, she remembered it in detail. Why would it have stuck with her, unless—?

He didn't get a chance to finish the thought. "I did come to see you," she rushed ahead. "But you . . . I thought . . . well, I don't know what I thought. That I was bothering you or something. You acted so . . . " Her hands fluttered up like a pair of wing-shot birds before falling helplessly back into her lap.

"Rude?" he supplied with a little snort of laughter.

She smiled at him. "That's one way of putting it."

"The truth is, I was crazy about you," he confessed, adopting the tone of a man much older and wiser shaking his head over the antics of a foolish boy. He didn't tell her that he'd been in love with her for as long as he could remember; that probably would have been more than she could handle. "I had it so bad, I was all bottled up inside. I couldn't even talk to you; I was too scared you'd guess. I know I must've seemed like a real jerk, but honestly, I didn't think you cared."

"I don't know what I could've done to make you think that. I always tried so hard to be nice," she said, frowning in confusion.

"I thought it was only because you were looking to make another conquest." Even as he watched her frown deepen into a scowl, he felt compelled to add, "In all fairness, can you blame me? All those guys hanging around you, doing handsprings to get your attention—don't tell me there wasn't a part of you that didn't enjoy it." If the caricature he'd done had rubbed her the wrong way, he suspected it was because she'd recognized some truth in it.

Her face relaxed in a small, grudging smile. "Maybe. A small part," she acknowledged.

"I also thought maybe the reason you were being so nice was because you felt sorry for me." At her puzzled look, he added with a dry, self-effacing laugh, "I suppose that sounds as if I'm flattering myself. The truth is, half the time I didn't think you even noticed me."

"Oh, I noticed you all right," she said. "It would've been hard not to."

"Why do you say that?" he asked guardedly.

"I don't know. You had a certain . . . quality. You always seemed to go your own way."

He smiled at the irony. "Me? I was wandering around lost most of the time. All I knew to do was to keep moving. Sitting still was a recipe for trouble in my house." He thought once more of Uncle Cole, and a shiver of loathing went through him. "Most people don't know this," he went on in the purposely casual tone he adopted whenever he discussed his family, "but you can get used to practically anything if you're forced to put up with it long enough."

"Then I guess I'm not most people." She looked him directly in the eye as she spoke. A veiled reference to her mother? he wondered. Practically everyone he knew had a story about having run up against the formidable Mildred Harvey at one time or another. It was said that Aldous Harvey, Elizabeth's father, had died purely in self-defense; it was easier than having to stand up to his wife.

AJ recalled his one, never-to-be-forgotten encounter with Mrs. Harvey, the night of his and Elizabeth's second grade play. After the curtain had gone down, while the other children were being fussed over by family members, he'd been standing off to the side, as usual, his grandparents nowhere in sight. He looked up at one point to find a large, imposing woman looming over him. "Where are your parents, little boy?" she demanded. He shrugged, suddenly tongue-tied, and she bustled off as if thoroughly disgusted by this sad state of affairs—or perhaps by AJ himself. In hindsight, he supposed she'd only been looking out for him, but at the time it left him feeling deeply ashamed and even more conscious of the fact that he was alone.

"No, you're not," he said, meeting Elizabeth's gaze. It was God's honest truth. She was like no woman he'd ever met.

She smiled, her gaze as compassionate as it was direct. "I don't mean to speak ill of your grandparents. I barely know them," she said. "It's just that they always seemed so . . . well, like raising their grandson wasn't the life they would have chosen if it had been left up to them."

"You're right, they wouldn't have. But that was only the half of it," he said, the old bitterness beginning to throb deep inside him like a rotten tooth he'd been doing his best to ignore until now. "You see, they never got over my mom's death. All they had left was me and my uncle. And God knows he was a disappointment to them. They tried in their own way, I suppose. I'll give them that. But with my uncle Cole, all they did was turn a blind eye. Whenever he got into trouble, they either didn't want to know about it or they made excuses for him."

"What kind of trouble?"

"Petty stuff mostly—drinking and carousing, that kind of thing. And women, there was plenty of that, too. Let's just say it wouldn't surprise me if I found out I wasn't the only grandchild." He gave in to a bitter laugh. "I'm just the one they had the rotten luck to get stuck with. Maybe that's why they didn't do anything to stop it when my uncle started beating on me."

"He beat you?" Elizabeth looked aghast. "Oh, AJ, I had no idea!"

"How could you? I never let on to anyone. Who would I have told? All it would've done was earn me another beating."

"How long did this go on?"

"Years. Until I was big enough to fight back."

"So that's why you—" She broke off, clearly not wishing to stir up any more bad memories.

"Why I set fire to his car?" he finished for her. "Yeah. But it's a little more complicated than that. Part of it had to do with you."

"Me?" Her eyes widened further.

"Cole saw some sketches I'd done of you from memory. He put two and two together, and from that day on he wouldn't stop pestering me. He'd go on and on about you having a boyfriend and how I didn't have a prayer of ever getting to first—" AJ broke off, continuing in a tight voice, "That, and other stuff. Things I can't repeat." He dropped his gaze, looking back down at the ground, at the bald patch where he'd plucked out every last living blade of grass. "I tried to ignore it, but it got so bad that finally I just snapped."

"Oh, AJ. I'm so sorry." He looked up to find her regarding him with an odd mixture of tenderness and outrage. "It should have been your uncle they locked up, not you."

"It could've been worse." AJ tried to make light of it. "At least it got me out of the house."

"Still . . ."

"Listen, that's not why I brought you here. I wanted to explain about why I acted the way I did. You see, somehow I got you mixed in my mind with all that other stuff, even though I know it wasn't your fault. In a funny way, I might even have blamed you. Because I don't think I'd ever have gone so far as to set fire to his car if it hadn't been for those things he said about you."

She nodded in understanding. "And when you saw me today, it brought it all back."

"Not at first. It wasn't until I was sketching you . . . " He shook his head slowly, trying to make sense of it himself. "I guess there's a part of me that wanted to get back at you for what happened. Not that I hold you responsible in any way. Please don't think that." He cast her a worried look.

"I don't." Her reply was as direct and straightforward as Elizabeth herself.

He remembered that she'd never been one to shy from the truth. He thought back to the time when their fifth grade teacher, Miss Jewell, had left suddenly in the middle of the school year. When their principal, Mr. Willett, had made the announcement to the class that Miss Jewell wouldn't be coming back, he'd been vague about the reason for her abrupt departure. All he would say was that it was "of a personal nature." That was when Elizabeth, age ten, had raised her hand to volunteer, "My mother says that Miss Jewell is going to have a baby. I don't see why she had to leave because of that. There's nothing wrong with having a baby, is there?"

"So you forgive me?" he asked, a smile teasing a corner of his mouth.

"There's nothing to forgive." She touched his arm, a feather-light brush of fingertips that acted on him like a jolt of electricity. "I just wish you'd told me sooner. I don't know what I would've done, but I wouldn't have sat back and kept my mouth shut, I can assure you."

"I don't doubt it." His smile widened. He found himself liking this side of her. She was as fearless as she was forthright, not at all the shallow temptress he'd shown in his caricature.

Right now AJ wished more than anything that he could take her in his arms. It was wrong, he knew; she belonged to another. But his emotions had always guided his course with Elizabeth, and they were doing so now, bumpy though the course might be. He stared at the water tumbling over the rocks as he fought to regain control. He'd learned the hard way that a single rash act can have long-lasting consequences, and he didn't want that to happen with her.

There was a brief moment, though, when he could have sworn she wanted him to kiss her. She was looking at him intently, her head tilted back a bit so that her throat was exposed where the top button of her blouse was undone, a pale column flickering with reflected light. A dragonfly stitched its way through the air over her head, iridescent wings flashing. The only sounds were the playful shouts of children in the distance, the cricking of insects, and the rushing of the creek.

AJ was kept from acting on his impulses by a deep voice booming, "Bets! Is that you?" He recognized it at once as Bob's. Bobby M, they'd called him in school, because he'd been one of several boys in their class named Bobby. The same Bob who was now engaged to Elizabeth. A sour taste rose in AJ's throat. He knew he should hate Bob. Through the years, he'd certainly tried hard enough. The trouble was, it was impossible to dislike the guy, even when he was poking his handsome head between the fronds of the willow that partially screened AJ and Elizabeth from view.

"There you are." Bob broke into a grin as his gaze fell on Elizabeth. "Say, I thought that was you I saw heading off in this direction. I said to myself, 'That fellow she's with looks a lot like AJ.' And darn if I wasn't right. Hello, my man. How the heck have you been?" Bob stepped forward, pushing the fronds aside and stooping to offer AJ a hearty handshake.

"Fine. I'm fine," said AJ, extracting his hand as soon as he could from Bob's enthusiastic grip.

"I ran into AJ at the fair, and we got to talking," Elizabeth explained, color blooming in her cheeks. "I hope I didn't keep you waiting, dear. We took a stroll, and I . . . I guess I lost track of time."

AJ doubted whether another man would readily buy such an explanation after coming upon his fiancée and a potential rival by themselves in a secluded spot. But Bob wasn't like other men. He appeared not to have a jealous bone in his body, a quality that arose not from stupidity or obtuseness but from supreme and, in Bob's case, well-founded confidence. Bob knew he had nothing to fear from other men. No one could touch him in terms of looks, charm, or athletic ability. He was not without ambition, either. Unlike many of their classmates who'd chosen farming over furthering their education, he'd gone on to college; he was at the University of Nebraska at Lincoln, AJ had learned when they'd run into each other downtown. Worst of all, Bob was nice. "A swell fellow" were the words most often used to describe him. In school he'd gone out of his way to be kind to those less well-equipped socially than he, and as captain of the football team, he'd always made time for those of his teammates in need of extra coaching. Even his attitude toward the boys with crushes on his girlfriend had been one of pitying bemusement, as though he'd found it perfectly understandable that they would be in love with Elizabeth.

"Haven't seen you around in a while," Bob remarked, dropping onto the ground beside AJ. "What have you been up to, my man?"

"Oh, this and that," said AJ with a shrug.

"AJ's just being modest," Elizabeth put in. "He's been making good money doing caricatures at county fairs. He's quite good at it. You should see the one he did of me. It was amazing how he captured my likeness." She flashed AJ a sly glance.

"That so? Why, you've been holding out on us, AJ." Bob gave him a comradely slap on the back, looking genuinely pleased to hear of his success. "We never knew you had a hidden talent."

That's not all you didn't know, thought AJ. "What about you, Bob?" he asked, eager to change the subject. "Looking to follow in your old man's footsteps?" Bob's father was an engineer. The reason AJ knew this was because his dad had worked at the same firm.

"If I don't sign on with Uncle Sam first." Bob leaned forward, elbows resting on his bent knees as he gazed out at the creek, momentarily lost in thought. He turned to AJ. "You hear about old Ricky Danforth?" Ricky was a boy they'd gone to school with. "Lost a leg at Inchon. Damn shame. I'd sure hate for it to have been for nothing. Let's face it, they need men like us over there."

"We need men like you here, too," said Elizabeth, her lips pinched in disapproval.

"My dad fought in the big one," said Bob, "and I'm not going to shirk my duty, either."

Bob would cut as fine a figure on the battlefield as he had on the football field, AJ knew. Looking into Bob's big, open, friendly face, with its eyes as blue and blameless as a baby's, AJ felt an odd affection well up in him. Affection tempered by a strong dose of envy.

"Even if it means leaving your girl behind?" he found himself saying.

Bob darted Elizabeth a sheepish look, his broad brow rumpled in consternation beneath the lock of golden hair that had fallen over it. "Of course that's a consideration." He gazed at her with devotion. "But you'd wait for me, wouldn't you, darling?" he said with the air of a man who had no doubts when it came to his bride-to-be.

"Of course I would. That's not the point." She addressed Bob in an affectionately scolding tone. "The point is that men like you always think—" She broke off to cry, "What in the world is *that?*" She pointed at a large, bulbous green object bobbing and rolling its way downstream.

"Looks like somebody's supper," said AJ, reminded once more of the stash of watermelons upstream.

"Too late for it now," remarked Bob amiably.

"Maybe not." Before either of them could stop her, Elizabeth was kicking off her shoes and wading into the stream, her skirt held high. The renegade watermelon was now snagged between a pair of boulders within fairly easy reach. But she hadn't counted on the strength of the current. She was in only slightly over her knees when it snatched her footing out from under her and sent her plunging, with a cry of distress, into a pocket of deeper water midstream.

AJ watched it all happen in the blink of an eye, and a split second later he was on his feet, shoes off, scrambling to reach her. He went plowing into the creek, mindless of the sharp rocks biting at his bare soles. He hadn't gone more than half-a-dozen feet when he felt the pebbled bottom drop out from under him. He might have been swept downstream along with Elizabeth, who was clinging to a rock a short distance away, if he hadn't managed to grab hold of a low branch jutting from the embankment. He called out to Elizabeth, who looked more startled than panicked. Behind him, he could hear Bob splashing after her, sending up spray that licked at the back of AJ's neck.

But if Bob was larger and more powerful, AJ was quicker and more nimble. He'd had to be in order to stay one step ahead of his uncle. Hanging on to the branch, he maneuvered his way over to a wide, flat boulder. He climbed onto it, then, using other rocks that were either protruding from the water or shallowly submerged, he cut a zigzagging, leapfrogging path toward Elizabeth. Many of the rocks were slick with moss and, should he have slipped and fallen, he'd have split his head open like a . . . well, like a ripe watermelon . . . but somehow he managed to stay upright, wobbling precariously here and there but never losing his balance altogether.

"Hang on, darling! I'm coming!" he heard Bob call in that booming voice that, if all else failed, was sure to bring the Shaw Creek volunteer fire brigade to the rescue. AJ darted a glance over his shoulder to find Bob half sloshing, half swimming his way toward Elizabeth.

AJ was the first to reach her. With a strength he hadn't known he possessed, he seized her under the arms and hauled her onto the boulder upon which he stood. For a moment they swayed in unison, locked in each other's arms, their bodies as tightly pressed together as pages in a book as they struggled to hold their balance on their precarious perch. Through her sodden clothing he could feel the soft pliancy of her flesh and the pounding of her heart against his rib cage. A wet strand of her hair clung to his cheek. However chilled she might have been, she felt warm to him. Warm and pulsing and alive after so many years merely dreaming of this moment.

If AJ hadn't been on a rock in the middle of a stream he'd have thrown his head back and roared with laughter at the irony of it: In all his fevered imaginings, he'd never pictured their first embrace quite like this.

The next thing he knew, Bob was upon them and Elizabeth was being scooped up in his brawny arms as though she weighed no more than a half-drowned kitten. "My goodness, what a fuss over nothing!" she cried when all three of them were once more safely on dry land, shaking themselves off and wringing out their clothes. She was putting on a good show, trying to pretend she hadn't been in any real danger, but AJ could see how pale and shaken she was. He also knew, from the look she shot him, that the only reason she was making light of it was to spare Bob, so he wouldn't feel bad about not having been the one to save her from a possible drowning. Another man might have taken credit for it nonetheless, but not Bob. He was too honest.

So it was AJ who set aside his pride and said, "Maybe so, but we'd have both been in for it if it hadn't been for Bob here." He clapped the bigger man on the shoulder. "Good work, man."

Bob's furrowed brow smoothed, and he broke into a grin. "You were pretty quick on your feet yourself. I'll tell you what, if we both end up in uniform, I'll want you watching my back over there."

"You think I'd risk my neck to save your leather hide?" ribbed AJ.

Elizabeth flashed AJ a grateful look, and he knew she wasn't thanking him just for rescuing her. "As for me, I promise not to go chasing after any more stray watermelons," she said as she shook out her wet hair. "Speaking of which, I guess we know now where they got their name."

They all laughed, AJ most heartily of all.

"Now, what do you say we head back and get into some dry clothes?" she suggested. "Mama will have a fit if she sees me like this."

To AJ, she'd never looked more beautiful. Her damp hair curled in inky tangles about her face and neck, and the warm sun had brought color back into her cheeks. Through the wet blouse pasted to her skin he could see the outline of her brassiere and her breasts swelling like ripe fruit over the top. It was an effort to tear his gaze away. To tear his mind, too, from the image of Bob touching those breasts, his large, square hands laying claim to her on their wedding night.

"Sounds like a fine idea," said Bob, slipping an arm around her waist as they started back up the path.

"In fact, I want you both to be my guests at the barbecue tonight. It's the least I can do after you saved me from practically drowning." She tossed a glance over her shoulder to make sure AJ knew he was included in the invitation.

But he'd already slipped away.

CHAPTER THREE

"*So that story* she used to tell us about Dad being the one to rescue her was all a lie?" Emily frowned down at the diary, from which Sarah had been reading aloud, as if it had offended her.

The two sisters were snuggling on the sofa by the fire they'd built, sipping what was left of the chardonnay from jelly jars they'd unearthed from one of the cartons. Everything else was packed and ready for the moving van that was scheduled to arrive first thing Monday morning.

"I wouldn't call it a lie, exactly," Sarah said, lowering the diary to her lap. "She just left out certain parts. She wanted Dad to be the hero." She turned toward Emily. "Was that so wrong of her? So what if it didn't happen exactly the way she chose to remember it?"

Emily smiled a little, no doubt thinking the same thing Sarah was: that their dad had been a hero regardless. "Remember that time he stood up in front of the town council and told them it was a stupid waste of money to build a community bomb shelter? That if the Russians dropped the bomb on us, the radiation would kill us even if the blast didn't?"

"Who could forget?" Sarah had been old enough at the time to feel mortified at hearing her father speak out in front of all those people, especially in an era when his was such an unpopular stance. "Mr. Oxandale accused him of being a communist. Imagine that—Dad a communist!" Sarah chuckled, taking another sip of her wine. Eventually their father had been vindicated and the shelter had sat dormant, gathering mold and scorpions, until finally, years later, it had been bulldozed under. There had even been an article about it in the *Bugle*, calling it one of the biggest boondoggles in the town's history. Now there was a playground where it had stood.

The sisters fell silent, gazing at the fire crackling in the hearth as they mulled over their mother's account of that long-ago day. The diary entry had given rise to more questions than answers. Who was this mystery man who'd captivated the young Elizabeth? All they knew about AJ, from what they'd read thus far, was that he and their mother had gone to school together and that he'd done time in juvenile detention for having set fire to a car belonging to an uncle described only as a "horrid brute" who'd deserved it. While their mother had written at great length about AJ jumping in to save her after she'd fallen into the creek and the feelings evoked by that incident, she'd only alluded briefly to earlier events. She obviously hadn't intended for her diary to be read—and puzzled over, in this case—by a future generation.

"What I want to know is, what did AJ have that Dad didn't?" Emily ventured after a bit.

Sarah sighed. "Who knows?" Did it even matter at this point? Their mother had clearly made the right choice in the end. "Whatever it was, it wasn't enough to keep her from marrying Dad."

"But what if she didn't marry him for love?" Ever since her divorce, Emily had been prone to dark ruminations about marriage in general.

"There are all kinds of love," Sarah said.

Emily drained the last of the wine from her jelly jar. "Still, I can't help wondering," she said. "If Mom was so crazy about this other guy, why didn't she marry him instead?"

"Maybe he wasn't the marrying kind."

"Or maybe Grandmother Mildred put her foot down." The sisters hadn't known their grandmother—she'd died when Sarah was little, shortly after Emily was born—but from what little their mother had told them, it was plain that their grandmother had ruled her household with an iron fist. If she hadn't approved of AJ, that alone might have been enough to nip any romance in the bud.

Sarah put an end to the speculation by pronouncing, "Either way, Dad was the better man. Mom must have known that deep down, even when she was infatuated with AJ."

Emily remained unconvinced. "Actually, it's kind of tragic when you think of it," she said, getting up to toss another log onto the fire. "I mean, if AJ was the one she *truly* loved."

Sarah shook her head in fond exasperation. Why did Emily always have to be so theatrical? "If she hadn't married

Dad, neither of us would be here," she reminded her sister. "Now, that would be tragic."

"Speak for yourself," Emily replied moodily as she stood idly poking at the fire. No doubt she was thinking about her own unhappy marriage, which had dragged on much longer than it should have.

"I don't think Mom ever regretted her choice." Sarah sought to bring some perspective to her sister's dark flight of fancy. "Even if she wasn't madly in love with Dad in the beginning, it deepened over time."

Emily, still wearing a troubled look, turned to face her sister, holding the brass fireplace poker clenched in one hand as if it were a magic wand with the power to shed light on the past. "Yes, but that still doesn't answer my question: Why *him* if she was in love with someone else?"

Sarah heaved another sigh and gazed down at the worn leather volume on her lap, its ink faded and its pages yellowed with age. "We won't know the answer to that until we read more."

Emily eyed the nearly empty wine bottle on the coffee table. "I think this calls for another drink."

Sarah shook her head. "Better not. Remember, we still have to drive home." Also, the next morning they had church, then the usual Sunday visit to the nursing home, for which they would need every ounce of their strength. "If I don't make it in one piece, my husband and kids will be in the same boat we're in now."

"Don't even think it." Emily replaced the poker in the fireplace stand with a loud clang. "Nothing's going to happen to either of us. I won't allow it. If we weren't around, who would take care of Mom?"

Sarah wondered what their mother would have had to say about their reading her diary. Would she have seen it as an invasion of privacy—was that why she'd kept the journal hidden away all these years? Or would she have been relieved to know the truth was finally coming out? Something else occurred to Sarah just then, something so dreadful it sent a jolt through her. "I wonder if Dad knew," she said.

"About AJ, you mean?"

Sarah nodded, feeling a little sick. "Didn't they all go to school together? And you know how it is in small towns. People talk."

Emily's eyes widened. "Oh, God. You're right—he must have known. Poor Dad." She shook her head pityingly.

"And to think of his never letting on all those years." It was almost more than Sarah could bear to contemplate.

"So you think he married her knowing she was in love with another man?"

Sarah thoughtfully fingered a page of the diary. "Since he can't answer that, there's only one way to find out." Reluctantly, part of her still not wanting to know, she turned to the next entry.

CHAPTER FOUR

Dear Diary,

I stopped by AJ's grandparents' house today. I knew I wouldn't find him there, but I wanted to know if there was a number or an address where I could reach him. Ever since he took off, I've been going a bit mad wondering if the reason I haven't heard from him is because he's still angry with me, deep down, or maybe upset because I didn't give him proper credit for saving me from drowning. Or, worse, if it's because he was in an accident. Isn't that the silliest thing? Imagining him laid up in a hospital with broken bones, or possibly in a coma, just because he hasn't called or written? Goodness! What a swelled head I have! Maybe that caricature he did of me was the real Elizabeth Harvey after all, and I'm just put out because he's not falling all over me like every other guy. As for his pulling me out of the drink, I'm sure he'd say it was only what anyone would've done. Hardly the act of a lovesick man. Even if he had a crush on me at one time, it's foolish to think he's still pining for me.

On the other hand, it seemed like we had a true connection. I'm not sure I can explain it. But I felt it. I think AJ did, too. If only I could talk to him again! There's so much I want to know.

∽

Elizabeth frowned at the steno pad propped next to her typewriter. Shorthand had never been her strong suit, and she was having trouble deciphering what she'd jotted down in her boss's office just minutes ago. Something about a consignment . . . or shipment . . . to a retail outlet in Peoria. Or was it Porterville? She heaved a sigh, glaring at the old Royal as if it were to blame. Which was easier than having to knock on Mr. Arno's office door and ask nicely if he'd mind terribly repeating it one more time, knowing her boss wasn't one to suffer fools gladly. Besides, Mr. Arno was a busy man. He ran Arno Fashions, the largest manufacturer of women's hats west of the Mississippi, which employed more than two hundred workers. The only reason she'd gotten this job was because Mr. Arno had owed her mother a favor: She had introduced him to his wife some thirty years ago. Certainly it wasn't because Elizabeth was a crack secretary, despite her diploma from Masterson Secretarial College in Lincoln. She had the capacity to become a whiz at shorthand and typing if she were to apply herself, but, in all honesty, her heart wasn't in it.

Her fondest wish was to become a wife and mother. It was all she'd ever really wanted, perhaps because she hadn't had much of a family life growing up. Her happiest memories were of the years before her father had become ill.

After his death when she was eleven, only she and Mildred had been left to rattle around in their big, empty house. Every holiday season, it felt as if they were simply going through the motions. Her mother would dutifully put up a tree and deck the house in pine boughs and holly branches, but it was never the same as when Elizabeth's father had been alive. She dreamed of the day she would have a house of her own, one that would resonate with the happy cries of children. In her mind, she could see the shining faces of those children gathered around the Christmas tree, or on Thanksgiving around a table laden with turkey and all the trimmings.

As for her future husband, there was no guesswork there. Ever since they'd started going together their junior year, she'd simply assumed it would be Bob. He, too, had expressed a desire for a family of his own someday. And there was no question that they loved each other. It was only a matter of time before they made it official. At least that was what she'd always thought. . . .

An image of AJ intruded. She pictured him as he'd looked that day, sitting beside her on the creek bank like some sleek-limbed mountain lion in repose. Since then he seemed to have vanished into thin air, leaving her to wonder where he had gone and fret over the possible reasons for his maddening lack of communication. Ordinarily she wouldn't have expected a chance meeting with a former classmate to lead to anything, but she'd felt a connection between them and thought AJ had, too. Clearly she'd been mistaken. Fourteen whole days, and not a word in all that time.

But who was keeping track? Didn't she have better things to do than ponder yet another mystery surrounding AJ? Tonight was the engagement party for her best friend, Ingrid, which should have been enough to occupy her thoughts. The women of both households, Ingrid's and Elizabeth's, had been in a tizzy of preparation. Ingrid and her family lived just down the street, and the two young women and their mothers had been shuttling back and forth for days. Mildred was advising Gertrude Olsen on the menu and décor, which left Ingrid and Elizabeth free to devote themselves to more important matters, such as what to wear. It was to be an elaborate affair, complete with the finest champagne from Torvill & Sons in North Platte and delicacies such as foie gras imported from France; there was even to be an ice sculpture in the shape of a swan (though it wasn't expected to hold up well in this heat). Everyone who was anyone in Emory had been invited, including the mayor and his wife. Naturally Bob would be there, too.

All week Ingrid and her sisters had been making sly remarks about Elizabeth being next in line. Last Saturday, while trying on gowns in Gold's department store during a shopping trip to Lincoln, Ingrid had predicted coyly, "I wouldn't be surprised if it turns out to be a big night for you, too. Just think, by this time next week you could be wearing a diamond ring on your finger." She'd paused as she was zipping up to admire the emerald-cut solitaire twinkling on her own left hand.

This seemingly lighthearted remark had sent Elizabeth into a mild panic. What on earth was the matter with her?

she wondered. Why wasn't she filled with joy at the prospect of becoming engaged? Bob was everything she could want in a husband: smart, kind, well-mannered, and good-looking in a manly sort of way that didn't rely on such enhancements as Brylcreem and the bespoke suits favored by Mr. Arno and the men with whom he did business. Why were her thoughts occupied more and more these days by a man she barely knew and who wasn't a patch on Bob?

And yet she couldn't seem to escape those thoughts. Over and over she'd replayed in her mind the moment AJ had hauled her, dripping, from the stream. She recalled how they'd stood teetering on the rock, pressed together as if in a slow waltz. In real time the moment couldn't have lasted more than a few seconds, but in the reliving, it seemed to go on forever. She could see droplets of sunstruck water, tossed by the current, sparkling in the air around them, brighter than diamonds. She could feel the water rushing over her feet and the firm pressure of AJ's arms around her. Part of her wished she could have remained on that rock, locked in AJ's arms, far from the predictable life she'd always known.

The day before, she'd paid a visit to AJ's grandparents in the hope of obtaining an address or phone number for him so she could thank him properly for having saved her life. Despite his claim that he wanted nothing more to do with them, she couldn't believe he would shut them out entirely. His uncle, yes, but Joe and Sally were his only kin. And she knew what it was like to be without a family. She had her mother, of course, but no one else. Only her grandmother Judith and her aunt Prudie, both of whom lived far away and seldom visited.

She'd found the Keeners' address in the phone book. They lived on one of the rural routes in Cement Town, as far in terms of grandeur from the neighborhood she lived in, with its elegant homes and tree-lined avenues, as Emory, Nebraska, was from Paris, France. When she arrived at the small, nondescript house not two blocks from the Keeners' store and within sight of the cement factory's belching stacks, Sally Keener answered the door wearing a worn print housedress, looking as faded as an old, rolled-up newspaper that had sat uncollected on the porch.

"AJ? How would I know where he is? I ain't seen him in years," she scoffed in answer to Elizabeth's inquiry. The old woman eyed her narrowly. "Whaddya want with him? You ain't in trouble, is you?"

"No, nothing like that," Elizabeth hastened to assure her, her face warming at the notion. "I . . . I'm an old friend. I was hoping to get in touch with him is all."

The old woman's expression softened, her washed-out blue eyes brightening a bit. "You get ahold a him, you tell him his grandma was asking after him, hear? He's a good boy, even if he did get hisself into a bit of trouble there a while back. Hopefully he's straightened hisself out."

Elizabeth was reminded anew of the beatings AJ had been forced to endure at his uncle's hands while his grandparents had stood silently by, and she replied with a sweetness that masked her outrage, "Oh, I don't think he needed much straightening out. He had plenty of that growing up, I've been told. You know how you can iron out almost anything if you hammer at it long enough?"

With that she'd taken her leave.

But she was still no closer to tracking down AJ. He could be anyplace there was a county fair, and in July, in the Midwest, that meant anywhere from the northernmost reaches of North Dakota to the Mexican border. Eventually he'd turn up, she knew. But by then it might be too late.

Too late for what? demanded a voice in her head. Her gaze dropped to her left hand, which if her friend's hunch proved correct would soon sport a diamond ring. She now approached this long-held dream with something close to dread. Yet if Bob were to propose to her, how could she say no? More to the point, what possible reason would there be to refuse him?

It wasn't that she didn't love him. Her love for Bob was something she took for granted, just like the air she breathed. Like the air, it wasn't something she thought much about, either. It was simply there, a simple fact of her existence. Less than a month ago she wouldn't have hesitated to accept his proposal; it would have been as natural as . . . well, as taking the next breath.

What had happened to change that?

The answer came to her with a dull throb: AJ.

It seemed impossible that someone with whom she had only just become reacquainted could have captured her imagination this way. But stranger things had been known to happen. Who would have thought her whole life could get turned upside down chasing after a runaway watermelon?

Reluctantly Elizabeth shook herself free of those thoughts to concentrate on the business at hand. The door to Mr. Arno's office was shut and the button for his phone line lit, which meant he was on an important call—but as soon as he got off, he would be expecting the letter he'd just dictated on his desk. If she didn't have it typed by then, he'd be justifiably annoyed. Just as he had been when she'd sent that check to the wrong address, and before that when she'd misfiled the paperwork for one of their biggest accounts. If she didn't shape up soon, no amount of persuasion on her mother's part would prevent Mr. Arno from firing her.

The prospect didn't depress her as much as it should have.

Her desk sat facing a long glass pane, which provided a view of the factory floor below. A brigade of blue-uniformed figures was hard at work operating the steam presses, cutting and gluing lengths of felt and shaping them on forms resembling large wooden eggs, and applying what Mr. Arno called "the furbelows." At one end of the factory stood row upon row of metal trees sporting finished hats waiting to be boxed and shipped. It made her think of a forest, foliated with feathers and faux flowers instead of leaves. That, in turn, led to thoughts of the weeping willow under which she and AJ had sat, sharing confidences and perhaps something more, on that hot Fourth of July afternoon when life as she'd known it had abruptly veered off course.

Her reverie was interrupted when her boss, a big-bellied man with his few remaining strands of white hair arranged as evenly over his otherwise bald crown as stripes on an awning, thrust his head out of his office to bark, "Where's that letter, Miss Harvey? I haven't got all day."

༄

Four hours later, Elizabeth was standing in the tiled foyer of the gracious red-brick Georgian Revival that was her home, giving herself a last once-over in the mirror before heading off to her best friend's party. She was pleased with the gown she'd chosen, a strapless one that flowed like poured water over her slender form, its gathered silk bodice a deep sapphire, with layers of voile in graduated shades of paler blue falling from its cinched waist. It was eye-catching without looking as if she were showing off, which was only fitting since this was Ingrid's big night. In the same understated vein, the only jewelry she wore were the dainty pearl-and-sapphire earrings that had been a birthday gift from her grandmother Judith when she'd turned sixteen.

Mildred Harvey stood before her, buttoning the brocade jacket that matched her brocade pumps. It was too warm outside for a jacket, but that wasn't going to stop her from wearing one. She wouldn't have dreamed of attending a fancy dress party, or any function, without being properly attired.

"You look lovely, dear," she said after a lengthy, purse-lipped inspection. "A bit too décolleté, perhaps, but I suppose that's the style these days."

Elizabeth felt suddenly self-conscious. But there was no time to fetch her wrap, which would have meant another trip upstairs. Her mother didn't like to be kept waiting. Anyway, she didn't think her boyfriend would disapprove of her dress being cut so low. Bob was always proud to show her off.

"Thank you, Mother. You look nice, too," she replied dutifully.

Her mother was perfectly turned out, as always. Her wardrobe wasn't up-to-date with the latest fashions, but her clothes were classics that never went out of style, according to Mildred. For tonight's party, she was wearing a navy Lanvin gown that had made its debut more than a decade ago at the opening-night gala of the opera house in Lincoln. Similarly, her flawlessly made-up face, once as beautiful as Elizabeth's but grown soft and lined with middle age, owed its artifice to an earlier era. Her dark-red lipstick formed a little bow above the natural line of her lips, reminiscent of the actresses of the silver screen, and her eyebrows were plucked as thin as fingernail parings. Her marcelled coif, unchanged since her debutante days, hugged her head like an embossed silver helmet.

"Come, dear," said Mildred, as though Elizabeth were the cause of the holdup. "I know Gertrude always says the party doesn't start until we get there, but even so, we don't want to be late." Her gaze swept over Elizabeth once more as they headed out the door. "Do stand up straight, darling. You don't look nearly as pretty all slouched over like that. Remember, a woman's true beauty is in her carriage. How do you think Ingrid got that ring on her finger? It certainly wasn't because of her looks."

Elizabeth was quick to jump to her friend's defense. "Ingrid's pretty in her own way." Maybe not pretty in the way Mildred defined it, but she was so full of personality that you didn't notice her flaws.

"All I meant was you don't have to be beautiful to get a husband. Though, of course, it never hurts." Mildred patted her daughter's cheek with a gloved hand. "Take you and Bob, for instance—"

"So you're saying Bob only loves me for my looks?" Elizabeth broke in before her mother could finish.

"Don't be silly, dear. He loves everything about you. But you have to admit a man like Bob could have any woman he wanted. You have to ask yourself, would he have been attracted to you to begin with if you hadn't been pretty?"

Her mother's words had the opposite of their intended effect: Instead of making Elizabeth feel beautiful and lucky to be so, they made her feel shallow and unworthy, the flirty-eyed temptress of AJ's caricature. But it was useless to argue—her mother always got the last word—so she said no more as they continued along the brick path to the driveway, where Mildred's car, a black Packard with whitewall tires, was parked. The sky was still light and the Olsens' house less than a five-minute walk away, but Mildred had insisted that they drive. Arriving at a party on foot, in her view, was strictly for the lower classes.

"You'll see when you're my age." Mildred opened the driver's-side door and slid behind the wheel, easing her posterior in first before swinging her silk-stockinged legs around in a graceful little arc: a model of comportment, as always, even in the absence of onlookers. "You take it for granted when you're young, but it doesn't last forever. Enjoy your looks while you can."

Minutes later, they were pulling up in front of the Olsens'. Ingrid's family home was also a Georgian Revival, only built on an even grander scale, with twice the number of bedrooms and a whole separate servants' wing instead of just one maid's room. Dirk Olsen owned stockyards which supplied half of the state's beef to retailers across the country, and Gertrude, the daughter of a Texas oil tycoon, was wealthy in her own right. Ingrid was the eldest of their three daughters, all with the same tomboy build and horsey features, which they'd inherited from their mother. "Not a beauty among them," Mildred was fond of observing, which was just as well; otherwise she might not have been on such friendly terms with the Olsens. It was a point of pride for her that, though she wasn't in their league money-wise, her daughter outshone all three of the Olsen girls put together.

Ingrid rushed over to greet them the moment they walked in, dragging Elizabeth into a corner of the thronged foyer while Mildred stood chatting with Gertrude at the door. "You look positively *sinful* in that dress! You're easily the best-looking woman here," Ingrid declared without a trace of envy. One reason she and Elizabeth were such close friends was because Ingrid didn't have a jealous bone in her body. Thanks to doting parents and now an adoring fiancé, she was confident in her lovability and saw no reason to wish for what she didn't have. She was one of the few among Elizabeth's female friends who were able to look beyond her surface beauty to appreciate her many good qualities.

Mildred wound her way over to the two friends as soon as another guest arrived to claim her hostess's attention. "There you are! I swear you girls are joined at the hip." She cast her daughter an arch look before turning to give Ingrid a bright smile. "You look stunning, my dear. That dress suits you to a T!"

Ingrid smiled and gave a little twirl in her peach-colored gown. "It does, doesn't it? But that's only because Elizabeth helped me pick it out. You know me; I'm hopeless when it comes to fashion."

Mildred brought her gaze back to Elizabeth, still smiling but more forcefully now, and suggested, "Dear, don't you think you ought to mingle? You mustn't keep the bride-to-be all to yourself."

After she'd grandly sailed off, as if to set an example, Ingrid murmured teasingly to Elizabeth, "You don't have to do a thing but stay put. They'll come to you." She gestured toward a group of young men, former classmates of theirs, who'd just arrived and were darting surreptitious looks their way.

"They don't appear to be in any rush," Elizabeth observed with amusement.

Ingrid snagged two flutes of champagne from a passing tray and handed one to Elizabeth. "That's only because they know you're practically engaged," she said. "But Bob's not here yet, so you're free to bat your eyes all you like. There'll be time enough to be dull and settled once you're married." Ingrid's brown eyes twinkled. With her dark-blond hair in a smooth chignon, wearing the gown that indeed suited her angular frame, she looked prettier than Elizabeth had ever seen her.

But Ingrid's teasing remark about becoming dull and settled struck a sour note. Elizabeth had always envisioned marriage to Bob as being like the movies she'd seen in which married couples were either gay and glamorous or cozily romantic. She'd never imagined it as being anything like the marriages of her mother's friends. Now she looked around her at the older couples chatting among themselves, most of them staid and not at all romantic-seeming. Would she and Bob be like that someday, just another stout, silver-haired couple bragging to people at parties about the accomplishments of their children, more interested in the offerings of the buffet than any delights to be had later on in the bedroom? She felt a shiver go through her at the thought and quickly downed her champagne, grateful for the heady rush of warmth it brought.

Just then, as if on cue, she caught sight of Bob coming through the door with his parents, both as tall and well-built as their son. All thoughts of being dull and settled were instantly swept away by the sight of him. He was so full of life, so positively vibrant with it, that he radiated a kind of glow, as if he had more blood coursing through his veins than ordinary men. Even in his suit and tie, he looked as ruddy as if he'd just come off the playing field. She watched him pause to greet Mr. and Mrs. Olsen. After chatting with them just long enough to be polite, he excused himself, quickly cutting through the crowd to Elizabeth's side.

"Wow. I'm not sure I can trust the other fellows with you looking like that." He gave her a long, admiring look before slipping an arm around her waist and leaning in to kiss her on the cheek. Her worries faded at once. Whether or not she was the prettiest woman at the party, she was certainly the most fortunate. "You look lovely, too," Bob said, turning to Ingrid, the perfect gentleman as always. "Rosy as a bride, and it's not even your wedding day. I just hope Jeb—" Ingrid's fiancé, Jebediah DeJarnatte III— "knows what a lucky man he is."

Ingrid's eyes glowed, and her cheeks went pink. Though a realist about her looks, she wasn't above being charmed by the flattery of a handsome man. "Speaking of my intended, I should go see if he's all right," she told them. "Daddy probably has the poor boy cornered, talking the price of beef cattle and boring him stiff. Why don't you two lovebirds find a quiet spot where you can be by yourselves? I'm sure you have lots to talk about." She shot Elizabeth a meaningful glance as she hurried off, and Elizabeth felt herself break out in a light sweat.

She and Bob made their way into the next room, into which most of the partygoers had drifted, pausing to exchange pleasantries with those they knew. Bob made sure to pay his respects to Elizabeth's mother, who beamed at him in approval, and not just because he was complimenting her on her dress. Never mind that his father was a midlevel engineer and his family lived in a house the size of the servants' wing at the Olsens'. As they stood chatting, Mildred basking in his reflected glow, even flirting a little, Bob might have been the heir to a throne. "That boy is going places," she would always say in excusing the fact that he wasn't in their social class. "He'll make a fine husband."

As soon as they could politely escape, Bob steered Elizabeth out a side door onto the porch. They settled on a rattan loveseat overlooking the garden, where a crepitating chorus of crickets could be heard and hydrangea blossoms the size of cabbages glowed like pale constellations in the light that spilled from the windows behind them. Elizabeth leaned into Bob. His hand, clasped about hers, was warm and comforting. She pictured them sitting this way years from now, a gray-haired couple taking in the night air, and it didn't seem so terrible all of a sudden.

"You're sweet to be so nice to my mother," she told him.

Bob flashed her an easy grin. "Not at all. I like your mom."

That was just it, Elizabeth thought, a small grain of irritation working its way into her complacency: Bob got along with her mother a little *too* well. It shouldn't have been a problem—quite the reverse—but somehow it was. She had a sudden unsettling vision of the three of them having Sunday dinner at her house, a practice her mother would no doubt expect to become routine once she and Bob were married. At the same time, she knew that if her mother had disapproved of Bob, they wouldn't be sitting here right now. Mildred would have found a way to get rid of him long ago.

"And she likes you," Elizabeth replied.

"Well, I should hope so. Seeing as how I'm going to be a member of the family." Bob spoke in the same mild tone as when observing that it was going to be another scorcher of a day or that the Cornhuskers had won their last game.

Elizabeth grew very still. It had been an offhand remark, not so different from ones he'd made in the past when the subject of family and marriage had come up, but it felt different for some reason. She recalled Ingrid's coy prediction and wondered if her friend knew more than she'd been letting on. Had Bob confided in her that he planned to propose tonight? She felt oddly panicky at the thought, and the fingers twined about hers, which moments before had seemed comforting, grew hot and sticky all at once.

Oblivious to her change of mood, Bob went on in the same mild tone, "In fact, I was thinking we might make this a double celebration. Not to rain on Ingrid and Jeb's parade or anything, but what would you say about us making the announcement tonight?" He turned to her, looking not so much hopeful as pleased with himself for having come up with such a splendid idea. In his mind, it was a done deal. All that was left to decide were the details. And why shouldn't he think that way? Had she ever given him a reason to think otherwise?

"Are you sure that's such a good idea?" She managed to get the words past lips that had gone numb.

He must have misunderstood, thinking she was only being considerate of Ingrid and Jeb, for he plowed on, "I was going to wait for your birthday to surprise you." Elizabeth's birthday was a little more than a month away. "But then I got to thinking, why wait? Our friends and family are all here, except Grammy and Grandpa—" Bob's grandparents were away on a trip—"and we already have their blessing. Heck, we've even got the champagne. Seems a shame to let all that go to waste."

Elizabeth looked into his ruddy, beaming face, and thought, *I can't.*

I can't say yes. I can't say no. I can't marry him. I can't lose him.

Her mind in a hopeless muddle, one fractured thought bleeding into the next, she abruptly stood up. "I'm sorry, Bob. I . . . I'm not feeling well. I really should go home. I'm sure it's nothing," she assured him at the look of concern dawning on his face. "It must have been something I ate." Not a lie exactly: She did feel dizzy from the champagne, and her stomach was in revolt.

Bob peered up at her worriedly. "You *do* look a little pale." An instant later, he was on his feet taking hold of her elbow, as if fearful she'd topple over. "You wait here while I go get the car." Though the evening wasn't working out as planned, he was doing his best to swallow his disappointment.

"No, please. I'd rather walk. The fresh air will do me good."

He deliberated, his natural protectiveness clearly at war with the part of him that always did its best to respect her wishes. At last he reluctantly conceded, "All right. If you're sure."

She squeezed his hand. "I'm sorry to spoil the evening. I'll make it up to you, I promise." She turned as she was stepping off the porch. "Oh, and darling? Don't say anything to my mother. I don't want her worrying."

"What do I say when she notices you're gone?"

She managed a wan smile. "Just tell her . . . I don't know . . . that we had a fight."

Bob chuckled at the absurdity of it. Neither of them could remember the last time they'd fought.

On her way home, teetering along the sidewalk in her high heels, which after two minutes had already made her regret having turned down Bob's offer to drive her, Elizabeth thought about the apology she'd have to make to Ingrid in the morning. She hoped her friend wouldn't be too sore and that she wouldn't see through Elizabeth's flimsy excuse and demand to know the real reason she'd left the party without even saying good-bye. If so, she'd have to lay it on thick. She also had to decide what to do about Bob's proposal . . . or their presumed engagement, as he saw it. Dear, decent Bob, who was so unsuspecting . . .

Lost in thought, Elizabeth didn't notice the car passing by until it slowed to a stop at the curb. It was fully dark out, and in the glare of its headlights, she couldn't quite make it out. At first she thought it was Bob coming to fetch her after all. Then she saw that it wasn't her boyfriend's dark-blue Buick but a battered green-and-tan Studebaker station wagon.

A head was thrust out the window, and a familiar male voice called, "Hey, lady. Need a lift?"

Elizabeth, her pulse quickening, squinted to get a better look. It was him, all right. That distinctive face, with its clean planes and lines. Those blue eyes, which ought to have been declared illegal, given their effect on her. That breezy air of recklessness, as if he lived so close to the edge that he had little to lose. What was AJ doing in this neighborhood?

she wondered. Had he been on his way to see her? The thought caused her heart to lurch in her chest, partly in delight at the prospect and partly in panic at what her mother's reaction would have been had he come knocking at the door when they were home.

In her senseless joy at seeing him, she blurted, "Well, for heaven's sake, where have you been all this time?"

He broke into a grin, clearly pleased to learn that his absence hadn't gone unnoticed. "Here and there," he replied with maddening vagueness. "I just came from the county fair up Kingston way. Funny I should run into you. I was on my way to your place to drop this off." His head disappeared back into the car. He resurfaced a moment later, clutching a rolled-up sheet of drawing paper fastened with a rubber band. He held it out to her. "I wanted you to have it."

She didn't have to look at it to know what it was: the caricature he'd done of her at the fair. "You certainly took your time," she chided, annoyed at him for no reason she could think of.

"I only just got back into town. Anyway, I didn't realize you were keeping track." He sat there, the engine idling and his arm hooked over the open window, grinning up at her in that infuriating way, as if he knew something she didn't.

"Who said I was keeping track?" She felt suddenly, inexplicably on the verge of tears. "It's just that when I didn't hear from you . . . " She let the rest of the sentence trail off, fearing she'd already said too much.

"Get in." It wasn't a request.

"What?"

"I said get in," he repeated in the same amiable but firm tone.

Elizabeth obeyed. Not because of her blistered heels or even because she feared a nosy neighbor would spy her chatting with a known miscreant. She obeyed because she couldn't *not* get into the car. It was as simple as that.

The interior of the station wagon smelled like AJ himself: a combination of worn leather, crisp drawing paper, and freshly washed clothing left in the sun to dry. He might have been living out of his car, but it was clean and uncluttered. Not painstakingly so—the knapsack and rolled-up sleeping bag stashed in back were testament to his itinerant lifestyle—but enough to give the impression of someone who took care of his things, not at all the sort to set fire to other people's cars.

"I would've dropped you a line, but I didn't know that you'd want to hear from me," he explained in a matter-of-fact tone. He dropped the Studebaker into gear, and moments later they were cruising along Grand Street, Hank Williams crooning softly on the radio about a cold, cold heart. "You look nice, by the way." He darted her a sidelong glance. "You on your way to a party?"

"On my way home from one, actually."

"Isn't it a little early to be leaving?" he remarked, glancing at the clock on the dash, which showed the time to be just a little past nine.

"It's a long story," she said with a sigh.

AJ didn't press for details, but she had the sense that it wouldn't come as a surprise were she to tell him that the story had to do with her and Bob. "Feel like taking a drive?" he asked instead.

She shot him an arch look. "You seem to have a habit of shanghaiing me."

"Would you rather I drove you straight home?" he asked in a tone that suggested he knew what her answer would be.

"And give you the satisfaction of thinking I'm afraid to go off alone with you? Thanks, but I'll take my chances," she replied smartly.

Soon the gracious homes and sweeping green-baize lawns of Grand Street gave way to the more modest brick abodes of the neighborhood where Bob's family lived. They passed through downtown, where the storefronts were shuttered and streetlamps lit, and soon they were on a country lane that rambled past cornfields and pastures, with only the occasional farmhouse to break up the monotony. They continued along it for several miles, eventually reaching the tiny hamlet of Cross Corners, midway between Emory and Shaw Creek. It wasn't much of a destination, its main drag consisting of a gas station, a few stores, and a seedy-looking roadside tavern called the Rooster's Nest. Elizabeth was surprised when AJ pulled to a stop in front of the tavern.

He turned to her. "You a fan of the blues?" The neon sign above the tavern's front entrance cast a reddish glow over his face that made him look almost devilish.

"I don't listen to much of it, to be honest," she told him. Her mother's taste in music ran to the likes of Perry Como and Peggy Lee—that and show tunes—which were the only LPs in their house.

"In that case, you're in for a treat. There's a guy in there who'll teach you everything you need to know about the blues." He hooked a thumb in the direction of the tavern, from which drifted the sounds of raucous voices and laughter and the tinkle of piano music. "I come here just to listen to him play. Come on, let me buy you a drink." He hopped out before she could give him an answer.

Waiting for him to come around and open her door, Elizabeth felt a tingle of anxiety mixed with excitement. She wasn't in the habit of patronizing such places, and certainly not in the company of disreputable young men. But there was something about AJ that made her inhibitions seem ridiculously prudish. So she smiled as he opened her door, and stepped out to take his proffered arm.

Elizabeth should have felt self-conscious walking into a grungy roadhouse dressed in her evening finery, but for some reason she didn't. A few of the patrons stared openly—farmers in billed caps, many still in their boots and overalls—but she paid them little mind. *This isn't happening,* she told herself. She'd stepped out of her life into a fairy tale, where nothing was real.

They found a table in back, where they settled with the beers AJ brought over from the bar. The piano player turned out to be an old Negro man, so shrunken and withered that he would have appeared mummified had he not been in motion. Listening to him play, his fingers flying over the keyboard and his head bobbing in rhythm to the music, she found herself tapping her toes. It was a lively number, like nothing she'd ever heard—not so much music as the pulse beat of life itself. Before she knew it, she was on her feet, twirling across the dance floor with AJ. She wasn't thinking about her blistered heels. Or her boyfriend. Or even her mother, who might at that very moment be launching a frantic search for her. It was as if a window had been thrown open inside of her, letting in a gust of fresh air that had blown away all the old fears and reservations clinging to her like wet sheets of newspaper. There was only the music and AJ.

They made an odd pair, the man in his well-worn Levis and old checked shirt with its sleeves rolled up and the woman shimmering in sapphires and satin, but if anyone was eyeing them curiously, they were unaware of it.

The next number was a bluesy one to which they slow-danced while the piano player sang the lyrics in an ancient, cracked voice. They swayed together, holding on to each other as though to let go would rob them of something life-giving, as not too long ago they'd clung to each other on a rock in the middle of a rain-swollen creek. She could feel AJ's breath warm against her ear, just as she had then, and the steady beat of his heart as he held her tightly to him, one hand pressed to the small of her back. With Bob, who was so tall that he towered over her, she always felt al-most childlike when they danced, but in AJ's arms she fit-ted perfectly, as though she belonged there.

One number melted into the next; they were scarcely aware of the passage of time. "Let's get out of here," he said when the piano player finally took a break. She nod-ded, not trusting herself to speak.

Outside, he took her hand as if it were the most natu-ral thing in the world to do so. When they got to where his car was parked, he leaned on it instead of reaching for his keys, drawing Elizabeth against him so they stood nestled together, her back against his chest. They didn't speak. They just gazed up at the starlit sky, her head tipped back against his shoulder and his chin resting on hers.

After a bit, Elizabeth let out a long, slow breath and said, "I wish we didn't have to go back."

"We could keep on going, but I reckon at some point we'd have to turn back." His voice was low and throaty against her ear, with a note of deep regret.

"Not if you were to kidnap me."

He chuckled softly. "I'd never get away with it. They'd lock me up for good next time."

"In that case, we could just run away."

"You don't mean that," he said in a more sober tone.

In response, she swiveled around so she was facing him. Then she did something she'd never done before: She kissed a man without waiting for him to kiss her first. She felt AJ draw in a sharp breath as their mouths made contact, one that gave way to a low groan as the kiss deepened. For Elizabeth, the kiss was equally electrifying. She felt as she had while they'd been dancing to the music inside—as wild and uninhibited as the little girl who'd once turned cartwheels on the grass and, fresh from the bath, run naked through the house, giggling as her mother chased her. She wondered what it would be like to have AJ make love to her and thought she understood now why Lady Chatterley had risked everything for this: because, in the moment, nothing else mattered.

She could have stood out there all night, kissing under the stars, but everything must come to an end at some point—even fairy tales. All too soon, they were on their way back to town.

It was shortly after eleven when they pulled up in front of her house. She was relieved to find its windows dark, only the porch light aglow. Her mother must still be at the party. Otherwise every light would be blazing and Mildred in a frenzy, wondering where she was.

At the thought, the pleasant spell Elizabeth had been under was broken. AJ's words came back to her: *They'd lock me away for good next time.* There was more than one kind of prison, she thought.

"Don't forget this." AJ handed her the rolled-up drawing as she was opening the car door.

"Thanks," she said, tucking it under her arm.

"Will I see you again?" His pose was relaxed, one arm resting loosely on the steering wheel and the other slung over the back of the seat as he sat facing her. Only his eyes gave him away as they studied her in the faint glow from the dash, glinting with some deep, unreadable emotion.

Elizabeth didn't know what to tell him. With the breaking of the spell had come the oddest sense of stepping back into her life—her life here, the life she would one day share with Bob—the way she might step into a familiar item of clothing. "I'm not sure that's such a good idea," she said.

"The best ones never are." His mouth twisted in a hard little smile.

She hesitated before coming to a decision. "Is there a number where I can reach you? In case . . . " She paused. In case of what? In case she decided she couldn't bear being apart from him after all?

He fished an envelope from the glove compartment and tore off one end, scribbling a number on it. "It's a rooming house where I bunk sometimes," he told her. "The landlady takes messages for me."

Elizabeth took it from him, hastily stuffing the scrap of paper into her pocketbook as though it were a piece of evidence in a crime. Moments later she was fleeing up the front walk.

It was only later, as she was about to climb into bed, that she remembered the drawing. She retrieved it from atop her dresser, where she'd dropped it on her way in, and slipped off the rubber band.

But it wasn't the caricature he'd done of her at the fair. This was a more lifelike rendering, drawn from memory, of her sitting by the creek, her legs outstretched and her head tilted back, eyes half closed, in a pose that was, despite its innocence, almost . . . *wanton*. Elizabeth stared at it for a long time, partly in shock and partly in sheer wonderment at his vision of her, so unlike the one she had of herself as she stood trembling in her thin nightgown. The sound of a car pulling into the driveway—her mother back from the party—finally shook her out of her stupor, prompting her to roll up the drawing and tuck it out of sight under the bed.

CHAPTER FIVE

Dear Diary,

I have a confession to make: I'm not sorry Grandma Judith broke her hip and came to stay with us. Isn't that an awful thing to admit? If Mother knew such a thought had entered my head, it would be a dark day in this house. And I do feel bad for Grandma, what with the pain she's in and her not being able to get around, truly I do. But at the same time, a part of me can't help feeling secretly relieved. Because it means all talk of getting engaged has been tabled for the time being.

Bob's been wonderful about it. The house has been in an uproar, what with Mother and I running up and down the stairs all day, fetching this and that for Grandma (who isn't the easiest patient, I can tell you!). He's always on hand to run errands for us, but other than that, he's been sensible enough to stay out of the way. I know he's anxious to get a ring on my finger before he goes back to school in a couple of weeks, and I want that, too—or I will want it once I've come to my senses—but right now I'm too confused. Ever since the night of Ingrid's party, I've been at sixes and sevens. I can't stop thinking about you know who. I wonder if he's thinking of me, too.

Sometimes it seems like I must have dreamed it. Other times it's as real as when I cut my finger and it bleeds. That's how it feels: like I'm slowly bleeding to death, only on the inside, where it doesn't show. I think about him all the time. I think about when we kissed and what else I wanted him to do to me. I'm afraid of what would happen if I were to see him again. I'm afraid of what might happen if I don't. Why can't I make up my mind one way or the other? Why must I torment myself?

Last night I did something foolish. I called the number he'd given me and left a message for him. I told myself it was only to let him know that he shouldn't expect to hear from me again. Isn't that ridiculous? Like eating half a box of candy before telling the person who gave it to you that you can't accept their gift. But, like I said, I haven't been myself lately. What more proof do you need?

I have to go now. The phone's ringing. Every time I hear it ring, I practically jump out of my skin, thinking it's for me. That it's him. Maybe this time it is. Maybe he got my message.

⁓

"It's for you, dear!" her mother called.

Elizabeth's heart kept time with the thumping of her footsteps as she pelted downstairs. Was it *him?* She knew it couldn't be Bob or her mother would have identified him as the caller. It couldn't be Ingrid, either. Today was the day Ingrid and her mother planned to drive into Lincoln to look at bridal gowns, and they weren't expected back until later in the afternoon.

Her steps slowed as she approached the bottom of the staircase. Directly below she could see her mother standing by the small bow-legged table that held the telephone, with the heavy black receiver in her hand. For the umpteenth time, Elizabeth wished it weren't the only telephone in the house. Mildred considered a phone in every room, as in the Olsens' house, a pointless extravagance. In answer to the argument that having to dash downstairs every time the phone rang meant risking missing an important call, she would always say, "If the person wants to talk to you badly enough, they'll call back. Otherwise it couldn't have been all that important." As a result, there was no such thing as a private phone conversation in their house. Elizabeth and Ingrid, when they were younger, had had to develop a code when talking on the phone. And any male callers, with the exception of Bob, would inevitably lead to a grilling that turned a simple phone call into an excruciating ordeal.

"Who is it?" Elizabeth asked with a mixture of hope and trepidation.

"Some young man. He didn't give me his name," her mother replied impatiently, clearly thinking the caller ill-mannered for failing to identify himself. She extended the receiver to Elizabeth as if it were a misbehaving cat dangling by the scruff of its neck.

Elizabeth took it without comment, holding it away from her ear, a hand cupped over the mouthpiece, in the hope that her mother would take the hint and make herself scarce. But it quickly became clear that Mildred had no intention of doing so; she was far too interested in listening in.

She cast a pointed glance at the receiver. "Well, aren't you going to see who it is?"

Elizabeth was left with no choice but to bring the phone to her ear. "Hello?"

"It's me." The familiar voice greeted her with a husky intimacy that emptied her lungs of air and brought her heart to a momentary standstill. She didn't know how to respond. An honest reaction would only raise suspicions in her mother that she wasn't equipped to deal with, while a show of indifference would give AJ the wrong idea—she knew she needed to nip this relationship in the bud but didn't want him to think she was heartless. She was spared from having to make that choice when AJ, who must have sensed something amiss, asked, "Is this a bad time?"

Elizabeth darted a nervous glance at her mother. Mildred appeared to be sorting through the mail, but her alert pose gave her away. "No, of course not," she replied in a sprightly tone designed to throw her mother off the scent. "How are you? I haven't seen you in ages."

"I'm guessing you're not alone."

"No, but I'm glad you caught me," she said in the same false, bright tone. "It's awfully good to hear from you."

"Same here. I got your message."

"Really? Well, it was nice of you to get in touch."

"I'm just wrapping things up here. I should be pulling into town in a couple of days. Will you be around?"

The mere sound of his voice was wreaking havoc on her nerves. A storm was threatening to break loose behind her tautly smiling expression. "Why don't we meet for a drink? Any day this week is fine. I get off work at five." In her panic, she'd have promised him the moon just to get him off the phone. She didn't know how much longer her crumbling facade would hold out.

"Okay. Let's make it day after tomorrow, then. Look for my car. I'll be parked outside the Rail."

She felt a moment's panic. The Brass Rail was where a lot of her old school chums went for drinks after work. The last thing she needed was for one of them to spot her getting cozy with AJ and tattle to Bob. But with her mind whirling, she couldn't come up with a better suggestion; she would just have to finesse it when the time came. "All right. See you then. 'Bye, now," she chirped.

No sooner had she hung up than Mildred dropped her pretense of reading the mail. "Who was that?" she asked with an affectation of mild interest that was in sharp contrast to the keen-eyed look she gave Elizabeth.

"Just an old friend from school." Elizabeth struck a carefully neutral tone.

"Oh? Anyone I know?"

"You might have met him, but he's no one you'd remember."

That much was true. Those whom Mildred considered socially inferior rarely registered on her scale. If she remembered AJ at all, it would only be as "that Keener boy" who'd gotten into trouble a few years back. "Actually, I don't know him all that well myself," she threw in for good measure.

"Well, *he* clearly knows *you*." Mildred arched a thinly plucked brow.

"You know how it is. People move away, and old acquaintances grow in memory. To be honest, I was just being polite. He's only going to be in town for a few days, so I didn't see the harm in meeting him for a drink." Elizabeth feigned indifference, but in truth she was nearly faint at the prospect of seeing AJ again.

She was turning to head back upstairs when her mother asked sharply, "Who is this person? You didn't tell me his name."

Elizabeth paused at the foot of the staircase, frantically casting about in her mind. If she plucked a name at random from her class roster, she wouldn't put it past her mother to track down the poor, unsuspecting fellow and expose her for the liar she was. Luckily she was saved from having to respond by her grandmother calling from above, with amazing vigor for someone bedridden, "Mildred? Elizabeth? Is anyone home?" As if they would have left her alone in the house!

Her mother heaved an exaggerated sigh. "Dear, why don't you run up and see what she wants?" If Mildred was a taskmaster, she'd come by it honestly: Grandma Judith had run her own household like a battleship. Even now, elderly and infirm, she was still bossing everyone around.

But for Elizabeth, this marching order couldn't have come at a better time. She raced upstairs as if eager to do her grandmother's bidding before Mildred could attempt to pry any more information out of her.

She entered the guest room to find Grandma Judith sitting up in bed. Enthroned against the pillows propped behind her back, she looked like a wizened potentate in her pale-blue nightgown and the matching quilted satin bed jacket draped over her bony shoulders like a cape. Elizabeth could see the pinkish contours of her skull through her white hair, which was insubstantial as smoke, and noted that the hands resting on the coverlet were nearly fleshless below their knobby wrists. But her grandmother had retained her dignity as well as some vanity—she was like Mildred in that respect. In the time it had taken Elizabeth to climb the stairs, she'd managed to apply lipstick, albeit not very successfully.

"Did you have a nice nap, Grandma?" Elizabeth was in the habit of addressing Grandma Judith somewhat formally. She hadn't spent enough time around her grandmother to feel comfortable with her in the way that Bob did with his grammy and grandpa, who lived just down the street from him. Grandma Judith lived in Omaha, some two hundred miles away, so Elizabeth had seen little of her while growing up. Mildred always claimed it was too far for Grandma Judith to travel, but Elizabeth knew that was just an excuse—the truth was that Mildred didn't get along with her mother. Otherwise wouldn't she and Elizabeth have made the trip to Omaha more than once a year? Sadly, the feeling appeared to be mutual—Grandma Judith didn't appear to have tender feelings for Mildred, either. Elizabeth doubted that her grandmother would have prevailed on Mildred to take her in after she'd broken her hip if her youngest daughter, Prudie, who lived closer to her mother, hadn't coincidentally been suffering from an attack of shingles that had left her bedridden as well.

Elizabeth didn't mind, though. She liked having Grandma Judith around and was happy for the distraction it provided at a crucial time in her life. She was discovering belatedly that the more she got to know her grandmother, the more she enjoyed her company. She also secretly enjoyed watching Mildred hop to whenever Grandma Judith barked orders. Her grandmother wasn't shy, either, about making her humble roots known—the daughter of poor Irish immigrants, she'd married a peddler, Mildred's father, who hadn't become successful until later on—a reminder that Mildred hadn't been born with a silver spoon in her mouth, however many airs she put on.

"Fine, thank you!" Grandma Judith was a bit hard of hearing and tended to shout.

"Are you feeling any better today?"

"I'd be fit as a fiddle if it weren't for this hip!" Grandma Judith shifted her weight on the mattress, wincing at the effort. "That, and my bowels—they're all stopped up."

"Should I bring you some more of those stewed prunes?"

"What?" The old lady cupped a hand to her ear.

"Prunes!" Elizabeth repeated more loudly.

"Heavens no. Remember what happened the last time? I was in and out of bed all day and half the night. No, sauerkraut's the thing. Works wonders for the digestion."

Elizabeth smiled at her grandmother's Old World ways. "I don't think we have any in the icebox, but I'd be happy to make a trip to the store," she volunteered. "In the meantime, how about a cup of tea?"

"Bless you, my dear. Don't know what I'd do without you," said the old woman after Elizabeth had fetched the tea tray from downstairs. However grouchy and domineering she was with Mildred, she'd been nothing but sweet

and placid with Elizabeth. Elizabeth watched as her grandmother took hold of her teacup with a trembling hand.
Despite her efforts to hold the cup steady, some of the tea
spilled onto the bed, eliciting a cry of frustration. "There
I go again, making more work for you," she said as Elizabeth dabbed at the spill with her napkin. "Take it from
me: Growing old is no fun. Enjoy life while you still can
because you're only young once."

"You sound like my mother," Elizabeth said, reminded
of Mildred's comments the night of Ingrid's party.

This time Grandma Judith maneuvered the teacup to her
lips without spilling a drop. She took a satisfying slurp.
"She happens to be right about that, but I wouldn't make a
habit of listening to your mother," she advised. "Otherwise
you'll be in danger of turning into an old stick like her."

"Grandma!" Elizabeth feigned shock, darting a glance at
the open doorway to make sure her mother wasn't in the
hallway. But it was impossible to suppress the giggle that
rose to her lips.

"What she needed was another husband," Grandma Judith went on, unabashed. "Being a widow is no excuse to
close up shop. It was too late for me after your grandfather
died, but your mother was still a young woman when your
father passed. And let me tell you, a busy social life is no
substitute for a good man. You mark my words, Elizabeth.
Life's too short to waste a minute of it. If that young man
of yours doesn't make you happy, then go out and find
someone who will!"

Elizabeth started at the astuteness of her grandmother's
words. Was it that obvious? Or was Grandma Judith simply

more observant than most? Not that Elizabeth was unhappy with Bob—at least, she hadn't been until now. In
fact, he was a far better person than she deserved. She
flushed with shame, thinking of how she'd deceived him.
Oh, Lord, how had she gotten herself into such a fix?

"I . . . I thought you liked Bob," she stammered.

"Heavens, child! I never said I didn't like the boy. He's a
fine young man. But it's not what *I* think of him that
counts. The fact is, you're not in love with him. Any fool
can see that." Grandma Judith subsided against the pillows
at her back with a sigh. Spent from the effort of dispens-
ing advice, she turned her attention to more immediate
matters. "Now, why don't you pass me one of those biscuits? There's nothing like a nice ginger biscuit to go with a
cup of tea, I always say."

❧

That evening Elizabeth went for a long walk after supper
instead of following her usual routine of playing cribbage
with her mother or taking a book up to her room. (They
didn't own a TV because Mildred considered television to
be nothing more than a passing fad.) Strolling past the
Simms's house next door, she noted that the hollyhocks in
Mrs. Simms's flower beds were in bloom. At the Ander-
sons', one door down, the garbage cans were neatly lined
up at the curb, and a gleaming new Cadillac was parked in
the driveway. She thought about Mr. Anderson. Occasionally she'd see him sitting in his car after he arrived home
from work, staring into space with a grim look on his face
as if steeling himself to go inside and face Mrs. Anderson.

Elizabeth wondered how anyone could live that way. Probably neither of them was very happy. They appeared content enough when out in public together, but who knew what went on behind those mild manners and patented smiles?

Elizabeth wondered if that was how it would be with Bob and her: a life in which they cruised along side by side but in different lanes, each with expectations that the other couldn't meet. Which was worse: to marry the wrong person for the right reasons or to be with the right person who was all wrong in every other way? Grandma Judith had made it sound so easy. But could you toss aside everything representing safety and continuity in your life purely for the sake of love? Wouldn't that love become gnarled and twisted over time, like a tree deprived of water, without those things to nurture it?

She didn't know the answer. She only knew that if she didn't come to a decision soon, the uncertainty would kill her.

She returned home pleasantly tired, having strolled as far as the reservoir and back. As she approached the house, she looked up and saw that the light was on in her mother's room. Mildred often retired early to do crossword puzzles or curl up with one of her *Reader's Digest* condensed books. The light was also on in the room next to Mildred's, where her grandmother was installed. Elizabeth paused at the base of the mulberry tree that grew beside the house, gazing up at the pair of glowing windows. It struck her as unutterably sad that mother and daughter, separated only by a single wall, should be so at odds that they preferred their own company to each other's. Was that how it would be with her and Mildred in the years to come? And what if she were to do something that her mother considered unforgivable? Would Mildred disown her entirely?

Her steps were heavy as she climbed the stairs to her room. The only thing to guide her way, glowing like a lighted window at the back of her mind, was the thought of seeing AJ in just two days.

She arrived at the Brass Rail at the appointed hour to find AJ's station wagon parked out front, as promised. But it didn't look as if they'd be going anywhere, at least not in his Studebaker: Its hood was open, and AJ was bent over fiddling with something in the engine. She felt her anxiety mount as she approached him. What if they were spotted out here by someone who blabbed to Bob? Would he be so quick a second time to dismiss it as a chance encounter?

As if sensing her presence, AJ straightened and turned to face her. He broke into a grin, jerking his head in the direction of the open hood. "Fuel pump—looks like I'll need a new one," he said with the relaxed air of someone accustomed to such mishaps. He pulled a rag from the back pocket of his trousers and used it to wipe the grease from his hands.

"Sounds serious," she said, her eyes on his long, supple fingers as he rubbed them clean.

"Nothing that ten bucks or so can't fix." He stuffed the rag back into his pocket and slammed the hood down.

"But I'm afraid it'll have to wait until morning. Gabe's is closed for the night." The Chevron owned by Gabe Corcoran was the only service station in town. "Now, about that drink . . . " Elizabeth felt herself grow panicky. "I was thinking it might be best if I took a rain check on that, seeing as how you wouldn't want it getting back to your fiancé. What do you say we go for a drive instead?"

Elizabeth nodded, weak with relief. "We could take my car." It was her mother's, actually, but she used it to drive to and from work every day. She could easily have afforded her own car with what she'd saved out of her paychecks, but Mildred didn't approve of young ladies owning cars. It caused them to become far too independent, in her opinion. And what would her mother have to say about a young lady stepping out behind her "fiancé's" back?

But Elizabeth was so eager to be alone with AJ that it was easy to shut out the voice in her head warning her that it would only lead to more complications. His eyes were bluer than she remembered, or maybe it was the last rays of the setting sun slanting across his face that made them appear so. She could see the faintest of lines fanning from their corners and felt as though she were catching a glimpse of the more mature man he'd be one day. She felt a pang, wondering if she'd have the chance to know that man or if this was as far as the road would take them.

"We could do that," he said. "Anywhere in particular you'd like to go?"

"Not really. Why don't we just see where the road takes us?" Her carefree words did nothing to ease the self-consciousness that seized hold of her as they strolled, side by side, to where her car was parked. Suddenly she wasn't quite sure what to do with her hands. They flopped at her sides like newly sprouted appendages to which she hadn't yet grown accustomed, the one nearest AJ jerking away as if from a hot stove when she accidentally brushed against him.

Soon they were cruising along the rural route just outside town. "Corn looks to be ready for harvesting," AJ observed as he sat idly gazing out the window at the cornfields rolling past.

She nodded in agreement. "Mr. Hathaway down at the hardware store says it's going to be a good year."

"Rain always makes for a good year."

"Well, it certainly was welcome after that dry spell we had."

Small talk. Was that what they'd been reduced to? Nonetheless, the meaningless conversation was a safe haven into which she gratefully retreated. Better that than unleashing the welter of emotions bubbling up inside her.

She kept a firm grip on the steering wheel, her eyes fixed just as firmly on the road ahead. Yet she had never been more aware of another human being. When she sneaked a glance at AJ out of the corner of her eye, she caught him regarding her with a bemused look, a corner of his mouth hitched up in a wry smile as if he knew precisely what was on her mind.

"Stop that," she ordered, feeling herself blush.

"Stop what?"

"Stop looking at me like that."

He feigned innocence. "How am I supposed to look at you?"

"You know what I mean. People will get the wrong idea."

He laughed. "What people? There's no one else around."

"I meant if there were. We wouldn't want them . . . thinking things."

"Why not? I have nothing to hide." He cranked his window all the way down, letting in a rush of warm air. The sun had dipped below the horizon, and brushstrokes of magenta, gold, and scarlet stood out against the darkening sky. Amid the gathering shadows, the rows of corn stretching for miles on either side were knitted into a vast, unbroken sea with no distant hills to stem its tides.

"You might not, but I do," she reminded him.

His mouth twitched in barely contained amusement. "Ah. I take it you mean your fiancé. So it's not enough that we're sparing him any gossip from us being spotted together in a public place? Now we have to worry about any spies who might be lurking among the cornstalks?"

"He's not my fiancé." The words slipped out. She'd intended to set him straight on that matter, but not until she'd made it clear to him, in as gentle a fashion as possible, that he shouldn't get his hopes up just because she and Bob weren't officially engaged. Now she regretted not only her lousy timing but having been stupid enough to mislead him in the first place. It must be obvious to AJ that she wouldn't have trusted herself with him had she not been "betrothed."

But he'd clearly misunderstood because he asked in surprise, "You told him about us?"

"No, of course not. We were never engaged in the first place."

"So why did you tell me you were?"

"I don't know."

"I think I do." She caught a flash of anger in AJ's eyes. "Wouldn't want some juvenile delinquent putting the moves on you. Lord knows where it could lead. And you with your sainted reputation to think of." Once again he'd misread her intentions. Or, in this case, put the worst face on them.

"It wasn't like that." Elizabeth was clenching the steering wheel so tightly that her knuckles had gone white. She was angry at herself for bungling things so badly, and it made her lash out at him. "Anyway, it's not as if you didn't know about Bob and me."

But what was there to know? Could she honestly say she felt the same about Bob as she had a few short weeks ago? She'd been attempting to rationalize her growing disenchantment by telling herself it was only natural, when a couple had been together as long as they had, for the excitement of the first months to settle into something more sedate. But was that really the case? What if this thing with AJ weren't some form of temporary madness but merely her heart speaking the truth?

"Pull over," he ordered.

"Where?" There was nothing but cornfields as far as the eye could see.

"There's a spot up ahead." He pointed to where the shoulder widened in a graveled turnabout.

As soon as she brought the car to a stop, he reached over and switched off the ignition. For a long moment neither of them spoke; there was just the ticking of the engine as it cooled and the sound of crickets taking up their nightly chorus. At last he climbed out, and she followed suit. She found herself standing at the edge of a drainage ditch, which ran alongside the cornfield it bordered like a neatly stitched hem. It was nearly dark, and visibility was limited with the moon not yet risen, but AJ had no trouble finding his way; he bridged the ditch in a bound, extending a hand to help her over it. In the suit and high heels she'd worn to work, she wasn't exactly dressed for such activities, so she wasted no time in slipping off her pumps, then her stockings, which she rolled into neat balls and tucked into the toes of her shoes.

They continued deeper into the field, the only sounds now the chorus of crickets and night birds and the rustle of cornstalks bowing to let them pass. The setting sun's showy display had faded to a glowing red line sketched along the horizon. Soon they found themselves submerged in a green-smelling sea under a purpling canopy of sky in which a handful of stars glimmered. The corn was so high she could barely see above it. There was no mistaking this for anyplace but Nebraska in August, yet she couldn't shake the sense of having been dropped into a foreign land.

At last they emerged from the field onto a grassy, tree-ringed knoll that bordered on a fenced pasture beyond which stood a barn and farmhouse, its lighted windows casting a soft glow over the shadowy yard, where they could hear a dog barking. The moon had risen, a great golden orb hanging low in the sky, seemingly close enough to touch. Elizabeth felt as if she'd been deposited back on known turf . . . none the worse for the wear but altered in some ineluctable way.

She turned to AJ, asking in a hushed voice, "Do you think they'll mind that we're trespassing?"

"They won't know. They're probably just sitting down to supper."

She pictured the family inside the farmhouse gathered around the table saying grace, the farmer and his wife and their children, heads bowed and hands clasped in prayer. She felt enclosed in that circle somehow, even though she knew what she and AJ were doing was wrong.

He took off his shirt and spread it over the grass for her to sit on.

She lowered herself onto the ground, and AJ dropped down beside her. Despite her earlier anxiety, she felt strangely calm. It seemed perfectly natural to be sitting there in the moonlight beside the bare-chested AJ. She bent her legs to examine the soles of her feet, which were caked with dirt. "My mother would have a fit if she could see me now." But she laughed as she said it, the threat of any reprisal from Mildred only a distant speck on her consciousness.

"What your mother doesn't know won't hurt her," he said.

"She has a way of ferreting things out."

"You worry too much." He turned to smile at her.

"You want to know something funny? I'm not worried. And that worries me."

AJ slipped an arm around her waist. They sat that way for a spell, gazing up at the moon that was like some enormous piece of fruit ripe for the picking, neither wanting to be the first to break the silence.

At last she dropped her head onto his shoulder with a contented sigh. "When I was a little girl, I used to beg my parents to let me sleep outside on nights like this," she reminisced. "My father would always give in. He'd help me set up the tent in the backyard so I wouldn't get eaten by mosquitoes and let me borrow his flashlight. After he died, that was the end of that. My mother was always afraid some stranger would carry me off in the middle of the night, like the Lindbergh baby."

"And so he has." AJ chuckled.

She cast him a coy glance. "Is that so? Well, in that case, sir, what sort of ransom did you have in mind?"

He crooked a finger under her chin, gently tipping it up to kiss her. She'd been breathlessly anticipating this moment, despite her earlier resolution to nip the affair in the bud, but it caught her by surprise nonetheless—not the kiss but the intensity of it. There was none of the initial tentativeness of last time. AJ laid claim to her with his mouth and hands as though they were already lovers.

They went on kissing under the benign, unblinking eye of the moon. When he lowered her onto her back, she was only dimly aware of the grassy turf rising to meet her; she could feel nothing but the sensations that were like a slowly winding passage taking her deeper and deeper into a forbidden realm. Even her body felt unfamiliar, a stranger's yielding to touches that from anyone else would have caused her to shrink in modesty.

Bit by bit, he removed her skirt and blouse and under-garments, each button and hook a small seduction in itself, pausing every so often to nibble and kiss and stroke the warm flesh underneath. When at last she lay naked before him, she felt as though she'd not only been stripped of her clothing but turned inside out, her innermost recesses laid bare. She watched as AJ hurriedly removed his own clothes. There was a moment, looking up at him silhouetted in the moonlight, a figure seemingly wrought by hammer and chisel out of something more durable than flesh and blood, that she was certain she was dreaming.

But if so, it was a dream she didn't want to wake from.

⌒⌒

They made love on the grass in a way that was both tender and urgent. Elizabeth showed no hesitancy, yet he was acutely aware that it was her first time and was careful to take it slowly. In a way, it was like the first time for him as well. He'd been with other women but no one for whom he'd had such strong feelings. How could he love another when he was filled to the brim with Elizabeth? She was the first thing on his mind when he woke up in the morning and the last thing he thought about before he went to sleep at night. It was all he could do not to come, too, when he felt her start to climax. Only by some miracle was he able to hold back until her shudders subsided and her body went slack under his. His own climax, after he withdrew from her, was almost secondary to the warm swelling of emotion that overtook him moments later as he gazed down at her flushed face and saw the look of rapture she wore; rapture mixed with a childlike wonder as if at the discovery of something whose existence she had believed to be a rumor.

They made no move to don their clothing afterward. They lay on the grass, as unashamed in their nakedness as the first man and woman, AJ flat on his back and Elizabeth curled on her side with her head nestled against his shoulder and a leg slung proprietarily over his. He could feel her rib cage rising and falling with each breath. He still carried the sweet taste of her on his lips, a taste like the nectar drawn from honeysuckle. He held very still, not wanting to break the spell.

His only wish was that he could make time stand still so they'd be caught forever in this moment.

It was Elizabeth who broke the spell. "So, where are you going next?" she ventured after a bit. He caught a note of anxiety in her voice, as if she were wondering when—or if—she'd see him again.

He replied casually, "Actually, I thought I'd stay put now that the season's winding down."

He felt her breath catch. "For how long?"

"Maybe for good this time. I'll see how it goes. In the meantime, I can always pick up work around here." That wasn't his only reason for staying put, but he didn't want her to feel pressured into making a decision until she was ready.

"What kind of work?"

"I've been offered a job at the cement factory. You remember Brad Lewiston from school? He's a supervisor there. Says they're shorthanded because so many of their men have been drafted. It's not exactly what I planned on doing for a living, but it's good, steady work. I can't spend the rest of my life on the road."

Abruptly she sat up. "The factory? Oh, AJ." He could see the dismay on her face and knew what she was thinking: that it was one thing for her to work as secretary to the boss in a hat factory and another for him to be toiling on the line amid the dust and fumes, just another cog in the wheel.

He sighed. It wasn't what he wanted for himself, either. Growing up in the shadow of the cement factory, he'd sworn to get as far away from it as he could. And he had for a time . . . only to come full circle.

It hadn't always been like this. Once he'd lived in a nice house with a lawn out front in a part of town where the air was clean and fallen leaves were the only things littering the sidewalks. His father had had a job as an accountant at an engineering firm. His mother had kept house. They'd had a little money saved and plans for the future. Then one sunny day while AJ was at school, his mom and pop had set out in the family sedan for the funeral of an old army buddy of AJ's father in Lincoln. Five miles outside town they'd been struck head-on by a flatbed truck that had spun out of control. They had both been killed on impact, according to the policeman who'd been among the first to arrive on the scene. Instead of the funeral in Lincoln, they'd attended their own funerals.

"Pay's good," he said with a shrug.

"Couldn't you make a living as an artist?" she wanted to know.

He gave a derisive snort. "What I do isn't art."

"No, you're good. You have real talent," she insisted. "You could get a job as an illustrator, if nothing else."

"The thing is, I'm not sure it's what I want."

"What *do* you want?" She dropped back down beside him, propping herself on one elbow, her head cupped in her hand and her eyes searching his face. Her mink-brown hair blended with the darkness around them, leaving only the pale cameo of her face, which wore an expression so serious, as she waited for him to reply, that it moved him almost to tears. That his future was of interest to anybody besides himself seemed nothing short of a revelation.

What I want is you.

He didn't speak the words aloud; they would only have frightened her. Instead he drew her close and kissed her lips. He'd have made love to her again right then and there but for what happened next. AJ glanced up, distracted by the panicked whinnying of a nearby horse, and saw something he'd hoped to never again see in his lifetime: flames flickering out of control.

The barn was on fire.

An instant later he was on his feet, Elizabeth jumping up, too. "Wait here," he told her as they threw on their clothes.

"No. I'm going with you." She looked up from tugging at the zipper on her skirt.

"You can't." He seized her by the shoulders, forcing her to meet his gaze.

The stubborn look she wore at once melted into one of regretful acceptance. She knew as well as he what the consequences would be were they to be seen together in this remote place, in their grass-stained clothing, looking as disheveled as the pair of lovers they were. Once the panic over the fire had died down, there would be talk, and that talk would inevitably get back to Bob. Her reputation would be in ruins and her engagement—or whatever she chose to call it—broken. Not that it wouldn't be the answer to AJ's prayers for Bob to break it off with her, but he wanted it done cleanly. No messy leavings to haunt them later on.

AJ raced down the slope, buttoning his shirt as he ran, and catapulted over the fence into the pasture beyond. By the time he reached the barn, the farmer and his wife had managed to lead most of the animals to safety. Horses and pigs and chickens and dogs ran in panicked circles about the yard, squealing and squawking, barking and whinnying. AJ pitched in at once—there was no time for introductions—working frantically amid the roiling smoke and flames to rescue the last of the pigs before the fire, mostly contained in the haymow for the moment, spread to the stalls below.

He was making his way out of the smoke-filled barn for the last time, a squirming piglet tucked under each arm, when there was a tremendous cracking noise and one of the rafters collapsed in a shower of sparks, sending a great gout of heat rushing at him like a locomotive. He staggered into the barnyard, releasing the piglets, which went squealing off into the night. He was coughing and slapping at the stray sparks that clung to his skin like biting insects when he heard the welcome wail of sirens in the distance.

Minutes later a fire engine pulled screaming up the drive. Then there was the clang of metal ladders being un-hooked and the slap of hoses hitting the ground. Firemen in turnouts swarmed the yard while the farmer and his wife, aided by AJ, herded the animals into the pasture. The fire was nearly out when AJ, bent over to tend to a lame goat, felt a hand on his shoulder.

"Nice work, son," said a ragged-sounding voice. AJ looked up into the soot-blackened face of the farmer.

"I'm sorry I couldn't do more." AJ coughed, turning his head to look up at the barn, now a charred ruin.

"You did what you could. We got the animals out at least," said the farmer, an older man with bristling gray hair, in which ashes were caught like snowflakes, and pale-blue eyes that stood out in stark relief against his black-ened cheeks. He wore a look that was a mixture of regret and resignation.

"Good thing I happened by when I did." AJ unwound a coil of baling wire from one of the goat's back legs—it wasn't lame after all—and it tottered off, bleating piteously. He straightened, passing the wire into the farmer's hands.

"You can say that again. You got here mighty quick, too. We're a good jog from the road." The farmer was peering at him now with an odd expression. "Say, don't I know you? You look awful familiar."

"No, I don't believe we've met," muttered AJ. He felt a familiar tightening in his gut and knew he'd made a mis-take in coming to the farmer's aid. But what choice had he had? He could hardly have sat back and watched the man's barn burn to the ground.

"Maybe not, but I never forget a face, and I know I've seen yours somewhere." The farmer's expression was less friendly now. He was staring at AJ with something close to suspicion.

Luckily AJ was saved from having to respond by one of the firemen appearing to steer them clear. Not a moment too soon, for seconds later what was left of the barn collapsed in a cloud of smoke and charred timber, sending a last fistfuls of sparks funneling up into the night sky.

AJ took advantage of the confusion to melt into the night, slipping away to rejoin Elizabeth.

CHAPTER SIX

Dear Diary,

Something dreadful has happened! The police took AJ in for questioning. It seems there's some suspicion about how the fire started, and they think he's the culprit. The farmer recognized him from his picture in the paper after that trouble he was in a while back. I'm the only one who knows for a fact that he's innocent. But he won't let me set the record straight. He says it'll only ruin my reputation, and why should we both suffer?

I've been sick about it. They don't have any evidence against him— how could they?—but even so, it kills me to see him dragged through the mud for something he didn't do, especially when he was only trying to help. He says it doesn't matter what people think, but it does matter. Around here you're guilty until proven innocent. Even if he doesn't go to jail, he'll be tried and hung by the court of public opinion. No one will hire him after this. He'll be lucky if he doesn't get run out of town.

I'm such a coward! I should never have agreed to keep my mouth shut. I should have gone straight to the police. If it hadn't been for Bob, I'm sure I would have. But I don't want him to be hurt, too. And he would be, terribly, if my part in this were made public. Poor, dear Bob. He's the most innocent one of all. His only mistake was falling in love with the wrong person.

※

The Rainbow, in the heart of downtown Emory, was a favorite local gathering place: a two-story complex that included a restaurant, bowling alley, and bar. It was the kind of place where couples with children could enjoy an evening out without having to hire a sitter, wine came in a carafe and beer in a pitcher, and conversation in the restaurant upstairs was punctuated by the muted clatter from the bowling alley below. It was also where Bob and Elizabeth went for supper every Friday night that he was in town. Bob always ordered the same thing, chicken-fried steak and mashed potatoes, while Elizabeth generally went with the special of the day. The evening usually ended with Bob taking the long way home, a drive that at some point would find them parked by the old train yard, abandoned since the highway had made it obsolete back in 1939 and the closest thing Emory had to a lovers' lane. They would sit in his car and neck until it was time to head home.

Tonight when Bob moved to put his arm around her, she edged away from him, letting him know she wasn't in the mood. "What is it, Bets?" He looked more bewildered than hurt. "You're not mad at me, are you?"

"Why should I be mad? What have you done to make me angry?" she snapped. She knew it was unfair to take it out on Bob, but lately she seemed to have little or no control over her emotions.

He eyed her somberly in the glow of the dashboard lights. They were parked along the access road by the railroad tracks, where weeds and wildflowers had sprung up and railcars lay about in various stages of disrepair. A lock of hair had slipped down over his forehead, which was furrowed in consternation. It touched her for some reason—he looked like Superman bent on saving the world.

"All I know is you haven't been yourself lately," he said. "Take tonight, for instance. You ordered the same thing as me. And you don't even like chicken-fried steak."

She'd only ordered it because she'd been too preoccupied with thoughts of AJ and the trouble he was in to bother reading the menu. "I thought it was time I tried something different. Actually, it wasn't all that bad." *If you liked your meat dipped in grease and cooked to the consistency of leather,* she amended silently.

"It wasn't just dinner," Bob went on in his slow, thoughtful way, like a lawyer presenting his case—which he planned to one day do for a living. "You're always too busy to talk when I phone. You've been distant in other ways, too. Frankly, I'm surprised you made time for me tonight." A note of hurt crept into his voice, but it was quickly replaced by concern. "Is there something wrong, Bets? You can tell me. Whatever it is, I want to know."

Elizabeth looked into Bob's open, trusting face, and it was like a knife through her heart. He was more than just concerned; he looked scared—scared that whatever was eating at her had something to do with him. She realized it was useless to go on pretending. She wasn't fooling anyone, and she couldn't bear seeing him this way. It was almost worse than knowing AJ was suffering because of her cowardice.

She had to tell the truth.

Elizabeth swallowed against the lump forming in her throat. "I'm sorry, darling." She spoke gently, lovingly, as if that could somehow minimize the blow. "You're right. I haven't been myself lately. And there's a reason for it. I didn't want to say anything until I was sure, but you have a right to know. You see," she paused to draw in an unsteady breath, "there's someone else."

"Jesus, Bets." He shook his head uncomprehendingly.

"I would have told you sooner, but I . . . I needed time to sort things out."

He gathered his wits and asked in a dull, shell-shocked voice, "Who is he?"

She hesitated, wanting to spare both men any further pain before replying in a small voice, "It's AJ."

"You're kidding, right?" The smile struggling to take hold on his face slid away when he saw that she was serious.

"I wish I were." She hung her head. "I didn't mean for it to happen. It just did."

The slackness went out of his jaw as shock gave way to anger. He let out a curse, adding through gritted teeth, "That bum! I should've known. I'm surprised he didn't set fire to my car while he was at it."

"He's not like that." She immediately jumped to AJ's defense.

Bob gave a derisive snort. "I think his record speaks for itself."

"You don't know the whole story."

"For Chrissakes, he burned the Findlays' barn down! What more proof do you need that he's a menace to society?"

"He didn't do it."

"Who did, then?"

"I don't know, but it wasn't AJ."

"What makes you so sure?" His eyes narrowed.

She forced herself to look him directly in the eye as she answered, "I was with him that night."

There was no need to spell it out. Bob understood what she was telling him: that this was no innocent flirtation. She watched the color drain from his face and a kind of dull realization settle in before he slowly turned his head to stare sightlessly at the shadowy jumble of rust-eaten railroad cars. They might have been the remnants of a lost civilization given how desolate this spot seemed right now.

"I'm sorry," she repeated. "I never meant to hurt you."

"How?" he choked. "How did this happen?"

"I wish I could tell you. I'm not really sure myself." She yearned to put her arms around Bob and console him, and at the same time she knew that to do so would only make this worse.

He whipped his head around, demanding, "Are you in love with him?"

She said nothing, letting her silence speak for itself. Bob let out a tortured moan and dropped his face into his hands. When at last he lifted his head to look at her, his eyes were bloodshot and angry red stripes stood out on his cheeks where he'd dragged at them with his fingertips.

Her heart ached for him, but she knew she couldn't stop until she'd told him everything. She had come to a decision tonight, one she'd put off too long. "I wanted you to know before I go to the police. I'm sure it'll be in the newspaper. People will talk. They won't know everything, of course, but they'll put two and two together." She shook her head, her eyes filling with tears. "I wish there were another way, but I'm afraid there isn't."

His face hardened. "Did AJ put you up to this?"

"No, just the opposite. He's the reason I didn't go to the police sooner. He begged me not to. He knew what it would do to me—to us."

He eyed her in disbelief. "You love him that much? Enough to throw away everything just to save his neck?"

She had no answer. Until now there had been no need to put into words what she felt for AJ. It simply was: a force she could neither explain nor deny. "All I know is this is something I have to do."

She looked out at the moths pirouetting in the muted glow of the Buick's parking lights. Frankie Laine was crooning softly on the radio—a love song. With a low growl, Bob switched off the ignition, silencing the music and plunging them into darkness. She turned to find him staring out at the darkened landscape, his hands clenched about the steering wheel as if negotiating a sharp turn.

"So this is it? It's over?" His anguished voice floated toward her. Bob didn't crack. He didn't weep. He just sat there with a stoicism that cut her more deeply than if he'd begged her to reconsider.

"I don't see any other way." She felt her eyes well with tears and bit her lower lip hard to keep from breaking down. Knowing Bob, he would have felt compelled to comfort her, and that would have been too cruel.

On the way home, neither of them uttered a word. When at last he pulled up in front of her house, she didn't get out right away; she placed a hand on his arm, wanting to communicate to him somehow that this was hurting her, too, and that she still cared for him deeply. But his arm was as unyielding as stone. He didn't react, even to flinch from her touch. He wouldn't so much as look at her.

She opened the car door and got out, saying in a small, choked voice, "Good-bye, Bob." She'd only meant to say good-night, and, hearing the finality of her words, she felt something give way inside her—the last bit of glue holding her together. When she reached the front door of her house, she had to pause to collect herself before going inside to break the news to her mother.

∽

Mildred was anything but stoic. If she'd been thrown for a loop when told of the breakup, Elizabeth's subsequent announcement that she intended to go to the police on AJ's behalf was the match that ignited the flame.

"It's out of the question," Mildred snapped. "I absolutely forbid it."

She was seated at the dressing table in her room, her hair in curlers. She wore her favorite cucumber-green dressing gown. Her face, stripped of its makeup, plainly showed the fear beneath her fury, which made her seem vulnerable somehow. That vulnerability tugged at Elizabeth more than any threats or entreaties. In that moment, she hated her mother for making herself the victim. For causing her to question even for an instant what she knew was the right thing to do.

"You can't forbid it." Elizabeth, perched on the end of the bed, sat up straight and squared her shoulders. She could see her reflection in the mirror over the dressing table, juxtaposed with her mother's, and hardly recognized the dark-haired young woman who stared back at her with such fierce determination. "If I'm old enough to vote, I'm old enough to do as I please."

"Nonsense! You'll do exactly as I tell you."

There was a note of hysteria in her mother's sharp command: Her control over her daughter was slipping, and she knew it. Wanting to reassure her that it wasn't the end of the world, Elizabeth attempted to appeal to her better nature. More gently, she said, "I can't just walk away from this. Didn't you teach me to always do the right thing, even when it hurts?"

"I didn't teach you to commit social suicide!" Mildred shrieked.

"This isn't just about me." For once Elizabeth held her ground.

"So you'd ruin your reputation for some . . . some miscreant who isn't fit to breathe the same air as you?" The expression on her mother's face was one of supreme outrage mixed with incredulity.

Ignoring the insult to AJ, Elizabeth replied as calmly as she could, "It isn't just my reputation that's at stake here." She could feel a tightness in her temples signaling the onset of a headache.

"Who cares what anyone thinks of that boy? He's made his bed; now let him lie in it. It's *you* who has everything to lose."

Elizabeth dug her heels in. "I don't care what anyone thinks of me, either."

"Don't be naive, Elizabeth. A woman's reputation is everything!" Mildred spun around on her stool to scoop a glob of cold cream from the open jar on the dressing table, addressing her daughter's reflection in the mirror as she began rubbing it over her face with quick, savage strokes. "Do you think Mr. Arno would have hired you if he'd thought you had loose morals? Do you think Bob's parents would have wanted their son to marry such a person?"

Elizabeth shot to her feet, her cheeks stinging as though slapped. "It's not up to them. It's not up to Bob, either. *I* get to decide whom I'm going to marry," she informed her mother. "And for the record, I'm not ashamed of anything I've done. I'm only sorry that Bob got hurt because of it."

"What about me?" her mother shrilled.

"How have I hurt you, Mother?"

Mildred spun back to face her, her eyes like slits in the mask of cold cream. "You have to ask me that? My God, isn't it obvious? How am I supposed to hold my head up in this town with everyone whispering behind my back, 'There goes poor Mildred Harvey. Did you hear about her daughter and that Keener boy?'"

Elizabeth eyed her coolly. "I thought it was *my* reputation you were worried about."

"Yes, of course. But I have mine to think of, too." Mildred slapped the lid back onto the cold-cream jar, wrenching it tight as if it were a neck she'd like to wring. "That boy is trash. He comes from trash, and he'll always be trash. Why sink to his level? Didn't I raise you better than that?"

Elizabeth bit back the angry words that rose to her lips. The events of the evening had left her so spent that she didn't have the strength for this particular battle. Instead she made one last attempt to appeal to her mother. "Don't you see? It's *because* of how I was raised. Remember how Daddy always used to say to never judge a book by its cover? I just wish you could know AJ the way I do. He's a good person. It's not his fault he got stuck with those awful people."

"I suppose you think I'm awful, too!" Mildred's voice rose to a hysterical pitch.

"Mother, please. Of course I don't think that." Elizabeth rubbed at her temples, where the headache was in full bloom.

But Mildred wasn't letting her off the hook. "Don't lie to me! I can see it on your face."

Elizabeth regarded her wearily. "You want to know what I think, Mother? I think you'd be better off if you didn't worry so much about other people's opinion of you."

"I suppose you think you're going to marry this boy." Mildred rose imperiously to her feet, tightening the belt on her robe.

Marry AJ? Elizabeth hadn't even considered it until now. During the countless hours she and Ingrid had spent discussing what sorts of weddings they would have, it had always been Bob with whom she'd pictured herself walking down the aisle. What kind of wedding would she and AJ have?

But her mother's implication that such an act would be the social equivalent of hurling herself off a bridge was more than she could take. "What if I am?" she tossed back.

Elizabeth steeled herself for another tongue-lashing. Or worse. Her mother was perfectly capable of throwing her out of the house and cutting her off without a cent. But Mildred just stood there, her face, shiny with cold cream, frozen in an expression that was an odd mixture of defiance and defeat. She looked tired and old.

"Whatever you might think, I don't wish the boy any ill." She sounded as worn out as she looked. "If he really is innocent, as you say, then of course he shouldn't be charged. But know one thing: He'll never set foot in this house. Whatever you decide, I want you to keep that in mind." Mildred's eyes flashed with some of her banked fire. When Elizabeth turned to go, she didn't step forward to kiss her daughter good-night, as she'd done every night for the past twenty years. As she headed out the door, Elizabeth couldn't have said who had the upper hand.

On her way down the hall, she paused at the closed door to her grandmother's room. She was hardly in the mood

for company, and she didn't normally disturb her grandmother at this late an hour, even when she knew the old
woman was up, but something compelled her to knock.

Grandma Judith must have known it was she, for she
called brightly, "Come in, dear!"

Elizabeth found her propped up in bed reading a maga-
zine. "I just wanted to say good-night."

"Nonsense," rasped her grandmother. "You want to
know if I was listening in. Well, I'm not as deaf as all that.
I heard enough to know what's going on. Come here." She
beckoned to Elizabeth, waiting until she'd lowered herself
onto the bed before continuing in a gentler tone, "I know
you're angry with your mother, and I don't blame you. But
you mustn't judge her too harshly. The reason she's so hard
on you is because she's terrified you'll make the same mistake she did."

Elizabeth eyed her in confusion. "What mistake was
that?"

"Marrying the wrong man."

Elizabeth stared at her, too stunned to react. She'd had
more than enough shocks for one night and didn't know if
she could sustain another. But morbid curiosity trumped
all else, and she couldn't keep from asking, "What are you
saying? That she didn't love my father?"

"Love him? Of course she loved him! If she hadn't, she
wouldn't have been so torn up when he . . . " The old
woman hesitated, appearing to debate with herself before
going on, "I don't mean to speak ill of your father. He was
a good man. But he had a weakness for women. It nearly
killed your mother when she found out. I don't think she'd

have left him—she wasn't in a position to do that. But she wasn't going to suffer in silence, either. She punished him in other ways."

Elizabeth had been too young when her father died to remember much before that time. But she had a vague recollection of sharp words exchanged by her parents and a certain tension in the air. She recalled, too, the expression on her father's face most nights when he came home from work, as if he were steeling himself somehow. Like Mr. Anderson down the street.

A great heaviness settled over her, and, as she sat on the mattress, she felt as though she were sinking into quicksand. She shook her head, murmuring, "Poor Daddy."

"It wasn't easy for your mother, either," said her grandmother.

"I wonder what would've happened if he hadn't died." Elizabeth couldn't help wondering, too, if her father's fatal heart attack had been in some way brought on by the strain he'd been under.

"They'd have gone on making each other miserable, I suppose." Grandma Judith seized Elizabeth's hand, her bony fingers tightening about it like a claw. "I don't want you to think badly of him. Some men are like that; they can't help themselves. I'm only telling you so you'll understand. Your mother wasn't always like this. Once she was like you. But it made her bitter and hard."

Elizabeth nodded slowly in comprehension. The mists were clearing in other ways as well. She understood now why her mother had been so keen on her becoming engaged to Bob. "So she thinks if I marry someone honest and upright who'd never cheat on me, that will make me happy?" she said with contempt. Not that she could imagine AJ ever cheating on her, either.

"You could do worse than that young man of yours," observed Grandma Judith, but there was no conviction in her voice.

"Even if he's not the one I love?"

Her grandmother's hand tightened, her clawlike fingers digging into Elizabeth's wrist. Her eyes, sunk in the basketweave of lines crisscrossing her face, shone with a brightness that made Elizabeth wonder if she was thinking about her own husband, Elizabeth's grandfather, a dashing war hero turned successful merchant who was said to have been the great love of her life. Her next words confirmed it.

"Follow your heart, child. It may lead you astray at times, but in the end it never steers you wrong."

CHAPTER SEVEN

"My God." Emily snatched the diary from her sister's hands, flinging it aside in disgust. "She actually broke up with him. Can you believe it? She *dumped* our dad."

"Except he wasn't our dad then." Sarah retrieved the diary from between the sofa cushions.

Emily slumped back, crossing her arms over her chest as her indignation gave way to a more contemplative mood. "I wonder what made him take her back," she said, gazing into the fireplace as if the answers to their questions could be divined from its glowing embers.

The bottle of wine was empty, and the Chinese takeout they'd ordered had long since been devoured. Gone, too, were the sounds that had marked the daylight hours—the friendly toot of car horns as neighbors greeted one another in passing, snatches of conversation drifting from the sidewalk, the whir of bicycles zipping by. Those sounds had given way to the stillness of nighttime, a stillness broken only by the sporadic barking of a dog or the occasional rumble of a passing motorist.

"She must have come to her senses and realized the mistake she'd made," Sarah ventured.

"Or decided to settle for second best."

Now it was Sarah's turn to grow indignant. "I would hardly call Dad second best!"

Emily turned to look at her sister. "All I'm saying is that it's obvious he wasn't her first choice."

The two sisters could agree on one thing: Their parents' love for each other had been genuine. But it was becoming increasingly clear that it hadn't always been that way, at least not on their mother's part. The diary left no doubt that at one time she'd been in love with another man. To make matters worse, Emily, to her dismay, was actually growing to *like* this AJ.

"Do you think Mom ever regretted her decision?" she wondered aloud.

"Oh, I suppose so, from time to time. It's only natural." Sarah's tone was so sanguine that it took Emily aback.

"Don't tell me you've ever felt that way about Jeff?" she asked, expecting Sarah to scoff at the idea. Sarah and Jeff argued from time to time—what couple didn't?—but theirs was as tight a union as any Emily knew. She couldn't imagine her sister ever regretting her choice of husband.

But Sarah shrugged, her mouth curling in a small, secretive smile. "Of course. Didn't you ever wonder what it would be like if you'd married one of your old boyfriends? Whenever Jeff and I have a fight or the sex isn't so great, I picture myself married to Tony Casanerio. Only Tony never gets cranky or grows a paunch, and the sex is always amazing."

"Tony Casanerio? From the tenth grade?"

"Don't laugh. He was pretty hot, as I recall. Anyway, I'm certainly not the only one who's ever felt that way—every one of my married friends has had the same fantasy. You must have, too, before you and Greg split up." Sarah elbowed Emily in the ribs. "Go on, admit it."

For the most part, Emily tried not to think about her marriage. But admittedly there had been times during those years when she'd wondered what it would be like with someone else. "Well, there *was* this one guy," she confided. "Remember Kevin Sloan, from my senior year? About a year ago, I ran into him in the supermarket. Talk about hot. Boy oh boy, did I have the major flashback."

"Does he know you're divorced?" Sarah never missed an opportunity to attempt to hook her sister up with likely prospects, but Emily had so far resisted her efforts. She wasn't quite ready, though she'd been tempted a few times.

"No, and he's not going to know. Unfortunately—for me, that is—he's married. Happily, from what I hear."

Emily's thoughts returned to their parents' marriage. Had it been truly happy, as opposed to merely content? Would their mother have been happier with AJ?

"Speaking of husbands, mine is probably wondering what's keeping me," Sarah said with a sigh. "What do you say we give it a rest until tomorrow?" She fingered the ribbon marking their place in the diary.

"Call and tell him you'll be a little while longer." Emily felt a sudden, urgent need to know the rest.

"Easy for you to say. You don't have anyone waiting for you at home."

"Ouch." Emily made a face.

Sarah was at once contrite. "Sorry, Sis. That came out the wrong way. Listen, I'll stay if you want. I'm sure Jeff and the kids can do without me for a couple more hours." She put a conciliatory arm around Emily, pulling her close—a bittersweet reminder of their mother. When Emily was little, she used to describe her mother as "comfy." Sarah was comfy in the same way.

"You don't have to," Emily told her.

"No, I want to."

"Are you sure?" Emily didn't expect her sister to give up family time just for her sake.

"You bet." Sarah smiled at her, letting Emily know she wasn't alone in wanting to see how this story ended. "How much sleep do you think I'd get, anyway, not knowing how Mom and Dad got back together?"

With that, she turned the page to the next entry.

CHAPTER EIGHT

Dear Diary,

Mother was right about one thing: Reputation is everything. Ever since the Bugle ran the story about the surprise witness who exonerated AJ, it's been the talk of the town. Oh, people are nice enough to my face, but the minute I turn my back, I can hear them whispering. You'd think I'd confessed to being the one who burned down the Findlays' barn! No one has actually accused me of being a tramp, but I know that's what they're thinking. And who am I to deny it?

The one everyone feels sorry for is Bob. They all think it was Bob who broke it off, with good reason, after finding out about me and AJ. I've said nothing to set them straight. Let the poor man have his dignity. It's the least I can offer him.

As for AJ, no one knows where he is, least of all me. He left town right after the police dropped him as a suspect. I haven't heard from him except for a couple of postcards from out West—one from Denver, the other from Reno. I'd be lying if I said it wasn't killing me. I lie awake at night, wondering if I'll ever see him again. He promised to come back, but how do I know he will? I can't help feeling a little angry at him for abandoning me at a time like this, but I also know that part of the reason he went away was to make things easier for me. He imagines I'll be better off without him. And in a way, he's right. Once all this talk dies down, things will go back to normal, I'm sure. Mother might even decide to forgive me. But what difference does it make when you feel like your heart's been ripped out of your chest? Meanwhile, I'm still a fallen woman.

∽

The First Episcopal Church was the last place on earth anyone would have expected fireworks. Sunday services were normally the dullest of affairs, as the elderly pastor, the Reverend Harmon Freimuth, tended to lose track in the middle of his sermons and ramble on interminably. Sometimes he'd hold forth for the better part of an hour, oblivious to the fact that he had put some of the congregants to sleep. (It wasn't unusual for those sermons to be punctuated by the sounds of snoring.) As a result, several families with young children had defected to the Episcopal Church on the other side of town; it was either that or endure the embarrassment of having to continuously scold one's children when they grew restless during Reverend Freimuth's droning.

But on the third Sunday in September, in the year 1951, the reverend wasn't his usual doddering self as he hitched himself, favoring his bad leg, into the pulpit and cast his stern gaze over the congregation. Watching him straighten his hunched back, wordlessly delivering the message, even to those seated in the farthest-back pews, that no snoozing would be tolerated during today's sermon, Elizabeth caught a glint of the fire that must have fueled him as a young minister.

"This morning's reading is from Leviticus, chapter nineteen, verse twenty," he commenced in his gravelly voice, an arthritic hand resting on the Bible that lay open in front of him. He slipped on his half-rims and, bending his balding head, began to read aloud from the passage he was holding marked with his finger. "'Whoever lies carnally with a woman who is betrothed . . .'"

Elizabeth felt heat spread through her cheeks. The passage related to concubines, but it seemed directed at her. She wasn't alone in thinking so, either, because she caught glances in her direction from several of her fellow congregants. By the time the reverend launched into his sermon, all eyes were on her.

"These are troubled times," he began, peering over his half-rims as if into the very gates of hell. "We're seeing many of our fine young men off to war, and while I know that takes precedence for many of you, let us not forget: There's a war on the home front as well. A war against the moral decay that has infected the youth of today. More and more young people are defying their elders, listening to rock-and-roll music, engaging in lewd behavior." Here he leaned forward, his gnarled hands gripping the lectern, his censorious gaze sweeping the congregation before coming to rest on Elizabeth. "Even fornicating outside the sanctity of marriage."

Elizabeth sat rigidly in her pew, acutely aware of being the center of attention. Her mother, beside her, drew in a sharp, hissing breath, and Elizabeth could feel waves of shame radiating off her like heat from the wood-burning stove that warmed the church in winter. Hadn't she warned Elizabeth about this very thing? And now it had come to pass. Elizabeth was learning just how much a woman relied on her virtue to get by in society. Without it, she might as well be walking around with a scarlet A on her chest, subject to the slights and insinuations, dirty looks, and cold shoulders of all those who placed themselves on a higher moral plane.

These past weeks had brought a flood of such indignities. Irma Chamberlain, in line behind her at the butcher shop, sniggering to her companion after Elizabeth had put in her order, "I'm surprised she didn't ask for one of the cheaper cuts." Mr. Carducci at the bank asking for proof of identification before he would cash her paycheck, even though he knew perfectly well who she was. Kate Nichols, who was on the community book fair committee with her, suggesting that certain titles be excluded—titles of a sexual nature, she'd added pointedly. Those were just the worst offenders. She'd lost count of all the unreturned phone calls, the so-called friends—who would have stopped to chat before—who only nodded in passing when she encountered them on the street, and the party and luncheon invitations that had dried up overnight. Nowadays, the only invitations came from men making unwanted advances, most of whom wouldn't have dared to do so in the past.

At home, it was her mother's scorn she had to endure. These days, Mildred barely tolerated her presence, letting her know with every cool word and look of disdain that she was skating on thin ice.

Elizabeth supposed she ought to consider herself lucky that she was still employed—for the time being, at least. Her boss had been away on vacation these past few weeks. Tomorrow morning, when Mr. Arno returned to work, she'd learn the status of her job. The best she could hope for was that the gossip hadn't reached him yet, but that would only buy her a day or two at most. Once he learned of her indiscretion, she didn't doubt that Mr. Arno, a staunch family man, would send her packing.

The prospect would have made her even more miserable than she already was, but she was too beaten down to fret about it much. With the rest of her life in tatters, what was the loss of a job? These days she could hardly concentrate on her work. All she'd been able to think about, while typing up invoices and filing paperwork, was AJ. Since her fateful visit to the police station, she'd seen him only once, the day before he'd left town.

They'd met for breakfast at a diner off Route 9, and when he'd told her he was going away again, she'd asked in what she hoped was a normal tone, "For how long?" She'd struggled to maintain her composure while poking listlessly with her fork at the scrambled eggs on her plate.

AJ was vague. "Hard to say. A few months, maybe more." They were seated by the window, and as he leaned to take a sip from his coffee cup, a ray of sunlight briefly illuminated his face, highlighting its angles and the tiny lines like brushstrokes at the corners of his eyes.

To Elizabeth, a few months seemed an eternity. "What about the job you were promised?"

He shrugged, letting her know what she'd already figured out for herself: The job offer had dried up. "Something else will turn up," he said. He didn't seem too worried about it. "One of the advantages of life on the road—there's always fresh territory," he added with a smile.

"You'll stay in touch, won't you?" Her voice sounded thin and anxious to her ears, that of a fretful child seeking reassurance.

"Are you sure you want that?" AJ gave her a long, searching look.

"Why wouldn't I?"

"I don't want to make it any harder on you."

She understood what he was saying and replied with a toss of her head, "You mean my reputation? People are already talking. Let them. I don't care." Brave words, but on the inside she didn't feel so brave.

"You should care." AJ's tone grew stern as he eyed her across the scarred Formica table. In that moment, he looked strangely formidable, his mouth hard and his eyes like rivets in a steel plate. "You have your whole life ahead of you. This'll all die down eventually as long as we don't give them anything more to gossip about. You'll marry Bob and live happily ever after. End of story."

She looked down at the scarcely touched food on her plate. "What if I want a different ending to the story?"

"You feel that way now, but once you've had a chance to think it over—"

She didn't let him finish. "I broke up with Bob," she informed him. At AJ's look of surprise, she added, "Yes, I know what people are saying, that he's the one who broke up with me. But I couldn't let him find out on his own. I had to tell him about us before I went to the police."

"Which I expressly asked you not to do." AJ sounded almost angry that she'd gone to the police against his wishes.

It wasn't the reaction she'd anticipated. She'd thought he would be happy that she had ended her relationship with Bob. A little gratitude wouldn't have hurt, either. Hadn't she saved him from possible jail time?

"You didn't honestly expect me to sit back and see you accused of something you didn't do?" she demanded.

"I'm a big boy. I can take care of myself." He forked up the last of his eggs and shoved them into his mouth, washing them down with a generous swig of black coffee, which might have been bitter medicine, judging from his grimace. She was reminded of the old, arrogant AJ who'd been such a source of aggravation all those years in school. "You, on the other hand," he went on, using the business end of his fork to make his point, "don't seem to get what's at stake here. Look at you. You have what I could only dream of growing up. Only someone who doesn't know what it's like to have nothing, to *be* nothing, would willingly throw that away."

"You sound just like my mother," she replied, hurt.

"Maybe you should listen to her."

"Next time I will!" Her eyes stung with the tears she was holding back. "In fact, if this is how you feel, I don't know why you even bothered to say good-bye. It's obvious you don't care about me."

She tossed her napkin down and started to get up, but AJ was too quick for her. His hand flashed across the table to grasp hers by the wrist, nearly overturning her coffee cup. His eyes met hers, and she saw the heat burning its way through the ice. At last she understood: He was angry precisely because he *did* care. Enough to want what was best for her, as opposed to them.

Her heart leaped, and in that instant she felt as close to him as when they'd lain naked together in the grass.

"I don't have anything to offer you. Not yet." He sounded as if he, too, were struggling to contain his emotions. The hand gripping hers loosened. With his thumb, he lightly stroked the inside of her wrist. "But I will someday. Then I'll come back for you. That much I can promise."

"I'll be waiting," she told him, as if there had ever been any question that she would.

But now, after weeks of receiving no word from him other than those few innocuous lines scrawled on the backs of postcards, she'd been left to wonder if he would keep his promise. The uncertainty, along with the slings and arrows she'd been forced to endure, had weakened her resolve. Had she really known what she'd be in for when she first headed down this road? If she had, would she still have had the courage to speak up in AJ's defense? She liked to believe she would, but maybe that was just wishful thinking. The fact was, she missed her old life almost as much as she missed AJ and would have done just about anything to get it back.

Anything but prostrate herself before hypocrites like Reverend Freimuth. *The old goat!* she thought as she sat seething under the collective gaze of the congregation. He had no business singling her out when he was hardly above reproach himself. Wasn't it a known fact that in his younger years he'd had more than a twinkle in his eye for the young ladies?

The same obstinate streak that had gotten her into so much trouble propelled her to her feet now. She wouldn't sit there meekly bowing her head while the minister rained down abuse on her. Whatever she'd done, right or wrong, it was no one's business but her own. "Excuse me, Mother, may I get by? I'm suddenly in need of some fresh air," she said loudly enough for everyone in their pew and those around it to hear. The pastor paused in the midst of his sermon, his gaze seeking the source of the disruption, but she didn't stick around to listen to any more of his ranting. Holding herself erect and forcing herself to walk at a normal pace, she made her way down the aisle amid the stares and murmurs of her fellow worshippers.

It wasn't until she was outside, away from all those prying eyes, that her strength gave way. Weak-kneed, she leaned against one of the fluted columns flanking the arched double doors to the church, closing her eyes and taking slow, deep breaths in an effort to calm herself. Oh, God, what had she done? Now she could never show her face in church again. Certainly not that church. She might not have a place to live, either, if her mother decided to throw her out of the house. She didn't even have Bob to go to anymore. Bob, who'd always been her rock. No longer could she pick up the phone and hear his reassuring voice at the other end letting her know everything would be all right, or look into his kind face and know that whatever happened, he'd always be there for her.

What had she done?

She was leaning back, eyes shut, when she felt a gentle hand on her arm. She opened her eyes to see Ingrid peering at her with concern. A wave of gratitude washed over her. She knew her friend had risked embarrassment in slipping outside to comfort her, and she'd never loved her more than she did then. If Ingrid had been making herself scarce since the scandal had broken, Elizabeth told herself it was only because she was wrapped up in wedding preparations.

"Are you all right?" Ingrid asked.

"I think so. I'm not sure."

"Nothing broken?" It was an old joke between them.

Elizabeth managed a tiny smile. "Only my pride."

"That was quite a scene back there." Ingrid tossed a glance over her shoulder at the church's closed doors.

"I know. Wasn't it awful? The way he singled me out? How dare he!" Elizabeth pulled herself upright, the shame and self-recrimination of a moment ago giving way to heated indignation.

"Maybe he did go a little too far," Ingrid acknowledged without seeming to share Elizabeth's indignation.

Elizabeth was too incensed to notice. "I'll say! Why, the old goat has some nerve. He's not the only one, either. All those people whispering behind my back? Most of them have no room to talk. Irma Chamberlain, my God, do you remember what a reputation she had in school? And that awful Mrs. Crenshaw and her do-gooder ways—I heard she was caught with her hand in the cookie jar with that last fund-raiser of hers. They're all a bunch of hypocrites, if you ask me."

"Does that include me?" Ingrid asked quietly.

"You?" Elizabeth belatedly took note of her friend's subdued demeanor. Feeling suddenly uneasy, she nudged Ingrid, attempting to coax a smile out of her. "Come on, Gigi, you know me better than that."

But Ingrid didn't warm to the use of her childhood nickname. Nor was she rushing to Elizabeth's defense as she once would have—like the time in their junior year when Sissy Carroll had nastily accused Elizabeth of making eyes at her boyfriend and Ingrid had retorted that she wouldn't have to worry if she bothered to make herself presentable. Now Ingrid merely stood regarding Elizabeth with a pained expression. "Do I? Lately I feel like I don't know you at all."

Stung, Elizabeth shot back, "How can you think that?"

"How can I not?" Ingrid sounded as if she were the injured party. "The way you've been acting lately, I hardly recognize you anymore. First sneaking around with AJ and not breathing a word of it to me. Then breaking up with Bob, the sweetest, kindest man who ever lived. And you expect me to understand? What is there to understand? From where I sit, none of it makes any sense."

"You're my best friend, Gigi. Of course I wanted to tell you," Elizabeth hastened to reassure her. "But I knew that if I asked you to keep it a secret, I'd only be dragging you into something you wouldn't want to be part of."

"Well, you've succeeded in doing that anyway, haven't you?"

"I'm sorry," Elizabeth replied, hurt. "I didn't know you cared so much about what other people thought."

"I care about *you*, you idiot," Ingrid cried, throwing up her hands in exasperation. "Don't you see what you're doing? You had everything a girl could ask for, but clearly it wasn't enough. And now look at what you've done. No wonder people are gossiping about you. What did you expect?"

"What did I do that was so terrible?" Elizabeth's voice rose on a wobbly, high-pitched note. "Was it that I fell out of love? Or that I lost my virginity to a man no one seems to approve of?"

"For heaven's sake! Someone might hear you," her friend hissed. Color bloomed in Ingrid's cheeks, and she cast a nervous glance over her shoulder.

Ingrid had always been a bit of a prude—the closest they'd come to the forbidden topic had been in vowing to wait until their wedding nights—but it had never gotten in the way of their friendship before. Now there was a wedge between them because Elizabeth had broken that girlhood vow while Ingrid would walk down the aisle with her virtue intact. But would Ingrid be so judgmental if she'd ever experienced true passion? She loved Jeb, but their bond was rooted more in shared values and deep affection. If she knew what it was to make love under the stars, to be so carried away that you were scarcely in your right mind, she would understand exactly what had driven her best friend to act as she had.

"What is there to hide? Everyone already knows what a sinner I am," Elizabeth tossed back.

Ingrid cast her a reproachful look. "This will all die down if you let it." Her outburst, though mild, had blown through her like a strong wind, leaving her somewhat in disarray. The curl had gone out of her mouse-colored hair on one side, giving it the appearance of a sagging hem, and her hat sat at a tipsy angle on her head: a trim little felt number, navy blue with a grosgrain ribbon from which a feather stuck out at an angle, that Elizabeth recognized as one of Arno Fashions'. Ever since they'd been little, Ingrid had been like that, always with a button missing from her pinafore or one pigtail undone even when engaged in quiet activities. Now she reached up to adjust her hat before opening her handbag and fishing out a handkerchief, which she used to dab at her throat. "If you go around causing scenes, you'll only make it worse for yourself," she advised, tucking the handkerchief back into her handbag and closing it with a decisive snap.

"Since when is it wrong to stick up for yourself?" Elizabeth demanded.

Ingrid flashed her a sharp look. "That's just it. You don't seem the least bit sorry about any of this."

Elizabeth was sorrier than her friend would ever know—sorry not for what she'd done but for the way it had played out—but she tipped up her chin, striking a pose at which she'd become so practiced these past weeks that it had left a more or less permanent crick in her neck, and replied defiantly, "Why should I be? It's not as if I owe anyone an explanation."

"Not even your best friend?"

"Oh, Gigi . . . " Elizabeth relented with a sigh. She couldn't deny that her friend had a point. Ingrid shouldn't have had to read about in the paper. "You're right, I should have told you."

"Yes, you should have." Ingrid was cutting her no slack.

"I meant to. But after Bob and I broke up, then that awful scene with my mother . . . " She paused to shake her head. "I was such a wreck, I guess I wasn't thinking straight. It was all I could do to go straight to the police before I lost my nerve. Then all hell broke loose. . . . "

Ingrid was silent, her reproachful gaze letting Elizabeth know that a phone call was the least she'd deserved.

"So does this mean you're going to ask me to turn in my bridesmaid dress?" Elizabeth asked in a joking attempt to get Ingrid to climb down off her high horse.

Ingrid replied stiffly, "I think that would be best, don't you?"

Elizabeth gasped as if she'd been punched in the stomach. She stared at her old friend in disbelief. This friend whom she'd always relied on, just as she had on Bob, was suddenly as much a stranger to her as she apparently was to Ingrid. Suddenly she could see past her childhood friend, standing there in her flowered dress, her prim little hat and gloves, to the matron Ingrid was on her way to becoming: married and respectable, more concerned with appearances than with old alliances.

Elizabeth, feeling sick inside, managed to reply with as much pride as she could muster, "Don't worry. I won't embarrass you any further." With that, she turned and began making her way down the steps.

◦∕◦

Mr. Arno returned to work on Monday. Elizabeth, still raw from the bruising she'd gotten from Ingrid, greeted him with forced cheer and for the rest of the morning kept her head down on the off-chance that he hadn't yet gotten wind of the gossip. She was filing some papers when he stuck his head out of his office to bellow, "Miss Harvey, would you step into my office, please?"

Her heart began to pound, and she broke out in a light sweat. Was this it? Was she going to get the ax? Part of her hoped she would just so she'd be put out of her misery. Her main regret was that if she were to be fired, she wouldn't be able to save up enough money for her own apartment, which she'd made up her mind to do following the fit her mother had thrown after church on Sunday. She would have to find another job, and who would hire her now?

Mr. Arno was on a call when she walked in. A big man, he seemed to fill up the office, reducing it to the size of a phone booth as he paced behind his desk, the receiver to his ear. Elizabeth, waiting just inside the door, felt her tension mount, the faint, rhythmic thumping of heavy machinery underfoot matching the beating of her heart. *Please, let's just get this over with,* she pleaded silently.

Finally her boss hung up and, as if he'd just noticed Elizabeth standing there, gave a little grunt of acknowledgment and waved her toward the chair opposite his desk. Elizabeth sank into it, smoothing her skirt over her knees. She'd brought along her steno pad, just in case, but didn't expect to need it. It came as a surprise when Mr. Arno, instead of firing her, asked her to take down a letter.

She would never know how she managed it. It was a miracle that she was able to recall any shorthand at all, she was so preoccupied. When Mr. Arno finished dictating, she didn't get up right away, as she normally would. She remained seated, eyeing her boss anxiously. What now? Was she off the hook? Or was he just biding his time before he sent her packing?

But Mr. Arno only asked impatiently, "Yes, Miss Harvey? What is it?"

"Oh, I was just . . . nothing." Flustered, she rose clumsily to her feet, accidentally dropping her steno pad. Quickly she bent to retrieve it. She straightened to find her boss eyeing her curiously.

"What's gotten into you today?" he growled. "You're jumpy as a cat on the Fourth of July. Was it something I said?"

"N-no, of course not," she stammered, her cheeks on fire.

"What, then?"

"I, uh, I was just wondering . . . " She lost her nerve and asked instead, "Did you and Mrs. Arno have a nice vacation?" Oh, God. Why didn't she just walk away? What was the matter with her?

"Fine, thank you," he replied gruffly. "If you can call two weeks of being holed up in a cabin with the in-laws a vacation. Take my advice, young lady, and don't get married until you're good and ready. Because you're not tying the knot with just one person—it's their whole damn family."

She was surprised that Mr. Arno would confide in her. It was the first time he'd shared anything of a personal nature. "I don't think I'll be getting married for quite some time," she told him.

"Now, why is that? I imagine a pretty young thing like you would have lots of offers," he remarked, his grumpy expression giving way to a more fatherly one. Mr. Arno had four grown children, three of them daughters. One for each of his remaining hairs, he liked to joke.

"I had a boyfriend, but we broke up." She felt a pang at the mention of Bob.

"Well, now, that's too bad. Though it doesn't surprise me. I hear you were a busy young lady while I was away."

Elizabeth felt the fire in her cheeks spread to engulf her entire body. So he did know. She waited for the ax to fall, but incredibly her boss appeared nonplussed. Maybe he didn't know the whole story.

"I can explain," she said.

"No need. It's all right here." He fished a newspaper clipping, which some helpful employee must have left for him in his absence, from the inbox on his desk: the article in which it was reported that AJ was no longer under suspicion for the fire that had destroyed the Findlays' barn due to the timely intervention of one Elizabeth Harvey, who'd been with him the night of the alleged crime.

"Oh. I see." She eyed her boss warily.

"No, I don't think you do. Sit down, Miss Harvey," he ordered, causing her to abruptly drop back into her chair. He planted his meaty hands on the desk and leaned forward so they were eye to eye. "To be perfectly clear, I don't give a hoot what anyone says. I think it was a damned fine thing you did. Not many people in your shoes would have come forward like that. Especially not under the, ahem, circumstances." As if taking note of her embarrassment, he added more gently, "I may seem like an old codger to you, but I was young once, too, you know. And believe me, I wasn't the only one feeling his oats back then. Any folks giving you a hard time, you can bet they were the ones picking the straw out of their hair when they were your age."

Elizabeth could hardly believe what she was hearing. "Does this mean you're not going to fire me?"

Mr. Arno harrumphed. "Fire you? Now, why would I do that?"

"I know the only reason you hired me was as a favor to my mother," she blurted.

He gave a knowing chuckle. "Well, now, I can't deny it. But if I know her, my keeping you on won't be the best news she's ever heard. Correct me if I'm wrong, but I'm guessing she's fit to be tied right about now and that my turning a blind eye to all this won't sit too well with her."

Elizabeth risked a small smile. "You seem to know her pretty well." Mildred was so angry she'd like nothing more than to see her daughter thoroughly punished and stripped of any last shred of dignity.

"Indeed I do. We go way back, your mother and I. And I can't think of a more fitting way to repay the favor she did me, in introducing me to Mrs. Arno all those years ago, than to keep her wayward daughter in my employ," he said, tipping Elizabeth a wink. "That way we're even."

❦

After her chat with Mr. Arno, Elizabeth was feeling a little better as she drove home, but as soon as she was within sight of her house, any hope of spending a peaceful evening holed up in her room vanished.

An ambulance was parked in the driveway, its lights flashing.

She felt a surge of panic, thinking something had happened to Mildred. Some injury or attack brought on by Elizabeth having wished in moments of anger that her mother could know what it was to suffer. But as she charged past the group of concerned-looking neighbors gathered on the lawn, she could see her mother on the phone just inside the open door, pacing back and forth with the receiver to her ear. She hung up as soon as she spied Elizabeth.

"Where have you been?" Mildred cried, rushing to meet her. "I've been trying to reach you!"

"What is it?" Elizabeth asked in alarm.

"It's your grandmother."

Elizabeth was seized with panic. "What happened? Is she going to be all right?"

"She's dead."

"What?" Elizabeth felt the foyer start to revolve as if she'd stepped onto a moving carousel.

"She was unconscious when I went up to check on her after her nap," Mildred went on in the same tone of barely contained hysteria. "By the time the ambulance arrived, it was too late. I tried calling you at work, but they said you'd already left. You were so long in getting here, I thought—" She didn't have to say it: It was written in her taut mouth and the set of her jaw. She thought Elizabeth had been with AJ.

"I came straight home," Elizabeth reported in a dull voice. As if it mattered now.

"Well, you're too late." A strange note, almost of glee, crept into Mildred's voice. Hectic stripes stood out on her cheeks, and her eyes glittered. "I hope you're satisfied. This is all your fault, you know."

Elizabeth was instantly shocked back into awareness. "Mother! That's a horrible thing to say."

"It's true," her mother persisted in a loud voice, heedless of the neighbors hovering outside the open door. "All the trouble you've caused. Her heart just couldn't take it."

Elizabeth knew that Mildred, in her present state, wasn't fully conscious of what she was saying. She also knew, from snide remarks her mother had let fall, that Mildred was jealous of the close bond she'd formed with her grandmother. But the hurtful words found their mark. Tears sprang to her eyes as she tried to push past her mother. "Where is she? Where are they taking her? I want to see her."

Mildred moved to block her path. "Haven't you done enough? Can't you just leave her in peace?"

Elizabeth was crying openly now, tears running down her cheeks unchecked. Logically she knew she couldn't have had anything to do with her grandmother's death, but she felt guilty nonetheless. Suppose all the tension in the household *had* taken its toll? Look at her mother—she'd aged ten years in the past few weeks. She appeared almost haggard despite the fact that she was dressed impeccably, as always, in a flowered shirtwaist and pearls, not a hair out of place.

"I want to see her," Elizabeth insisted.

She'd just started up the stairs when a pair of white-jacketed ambulance attendants appeared on the landing above, bearing a stretcher. She retreated, watching in dull-eyed disbelief as they carried it down, her gaze fixed on the lifeless, blanket-covered form strapped to it. In a kind of daze, she followed the attendants outside, where they loaded the stretcher into the ambulance before taking off. Not until the ambulance was disappearing around the corner onto Maple Drive—the route to the funeral home— did she realize she'd neglected to say a final good-bye.

Now it was too late.

It all came over her in a rush like a tidal wave: everything she'd lost. And now her grandmother, too.

Their next-door neighbor, Dottie Simms, came over and put an arm around her. Dottie was around the same age as Mildred, but any similarities between the two women ended there. Where Mildred tended to put on airs, Dottie was down-to-earth, happiest puttering around in her yard in a pair of baggy dungarees and an old shirt of her husband's. When she wasn't gardening, she was cooking for her family. Growing up, Elizabeth had often been lured over to the Simmses' house by the heavenly smells wafting from the kitchen. It was Mrs. Simms who'd provided homemade cookies and, when need be, a sympathetic ear, neither of which Elizabeth had ever gotten from her mother.

But right now her neighbor's sympathy was harder to bear than her mother's scorn. She felt herself stiffen as

Mrs. Simms murmured kindly, "Go on, dear, have yourself a good cry. You'll feel better."

Nothing is going to make me feel better, she thought. Nearly everyone she'd ever cared about was gone: her father, Bob, Ingrid, her grandmother. AJ, too, whom she was certain she would never see again.

Without a word, she took off down the sidewalk. She walked at a brisk pace, not running but not slowing, either, when it started to drizzle. She didn't know where she was headed, nor did she care. By the time she reached the main thoroughfare into town, the rain was coming down hard, lashing at her in waves. Even then, she kept going, mindless of the fact that she was soaked to the skin. She walked all the way into town and beyond, where the main drag became a residential street lined with modest homes. She followed it for more than a mile until the homes gave way to farmlands. A few motorists stopped to ask if she wanted a ride, but she waved them on. Even with her feet blistered and her clothing drenched, she had no wish for an audience to her misery.

She was nearing the turnoff to Shaw Creek when a familiar blue-and-cream Buick coupe slowed onto the shoulder just ahead of her, sending a rooster-comb of muddy water spraying from its back tires. The window on the driver's side rolled down, and a familiar blond head thrust its way out to shout above the pounding of the rain, "For God's sake, Bets, get in before you catch your death!"

∽

"How did you know where to find me?" she asked as she sat huddled in the front seat of Bob's car.

He was bent over, fiddling with the dial on the heater. "Just luck, I guess."

"Did my mother send you?"

"No. She only called to tell me that you'd left the house pretty upset and that she didn't know where you'd gone." He straightened to eye her solemnly. "I'm sorry about your grandma, Bets."

"Thanks." She began to shiver in earnest.

"It was my idea to go looking for you," he went on. "I just didn't expect to find you all the way out here, half drowned. Here, put this on." He removed his jacket and draped it over her shoulders.

"I'll get it all wet," she protested.

"It doesn't matter. I won't be needing it after tomorrow."

"Why? What's tomorrow?"

"I leave for Fort Riley in the morning."

"You enlisted?" She gaped at him in astonishment.

He smiled and said, "Does that surprise you? I told you I was going to."

"I didn't think you'd actually go through with it."

"Well, I did."

"What about school? I thought you were going to wait until after graduation."

"Things have changed." He looked past her, the muscles in his jaw tightening.

This is all my fault, she thought. *I drove him to it.*

She gave a small, choked cry. "Oh, Bob." Suddenly it was all too much.

But he was quick to ward off a discussion, saying in a brisk tone, "Let's get you home and into some dry clothes. You must be chilled to the bone." He put the car into gear and checked for oncoming traffic before pulling cautiously back onto the road.

"Not home. Please, anywhere but there," she managed to reply through clenched, chattering teeth. She couldn't bear it after the awful things her mother had said to her.

"We could go to Grammy and Grandpa's, I suppose," he offered somewhat hesitantly. She remembered his mentioning some time ago that he'd be housesitting for his grandparents the week before school started. Presumably they were still in Omaha, where his grandfather had been scheduled for knee surgery.

She understood how difficult this must be for Bob and was quick to assure him, "Just until I dry off." After a moment, she inquired politely, "Your grandpa's okay? Did the operation go well?"

"Without a hitch. Grandpa says the old knee's better than ever and that it's the physical therapy that'll be the death of him." Bob caught himself and winced at the unfortunate choice of words. "Sorry."

But Elizabeth remembered that above all else, her grandmother had had a sense of humor, so she managed a small smile. "You'll send him my best, won't you?"

"Sure I will." Bob fell silent, as if at the reminder that they were no longer a couple. In days past she wouldn't have had to send her best wishes; she'd have been delivering them in person.

Half an hour later they were seated at the kitchen table in his grandparents' modest brick house on Woodrow

Lane, Elizabeth wearing an old woolen sweater of Bob's and a pair of his grandmother's slacks that was several sizes too big. The sweater bagged nearly to her knees, and the only thing holding up the slacks was the belt buckled on its last notch around her waist. Her wet clothes were in the dryer in the laundry room off the kitchen. Faintly, she could hear the ticking sound made by the buttons on her dress as it went around and around in the metal drum.

Bob had made them hot cocoa, and now, sipping from her mug, Elizabeth felt the knotted muscles in her neck and shoulders start to loosen. She found herself thinking of all the meals she'd eaten with Bob's family over the years. From his mother and grandmother, she'd learned how to prepare all of Bob's favorite foods. From his father, an avid bird-watcher, she'd learned to distinguish the various kinds of birds that flocked around the feeder he'd erected outside their kitchen window. The truth was, she felt more at home here and at Bob's parents' house than at her own.

"How did your folks take it when you told them you enlisted?" she asked, thinking of how worried they must be at the very real possibility that he'd see combat.

"Pretty well," he said, slowly stirring his cocoa with his spoon while he waited for it to cool. She remembered that he liked it almost lukewarm, a legacy from when he'd burned his tongue as a child. "They'll be sad to see me go, of course, but they're proud that I'm serving my country."

"What time do you leave in the morning?"

"First thing."

"And after that?"

"Six weeks of basic training. Then I'll most likely be shipping out to Korea, as soon as they assign me to a unit."

Elizabeth felt fearful at the thought. So many men had already lost their lives or been gravely injured in the war; several were boys whom she'd known in school. It worried her to think of Bob being in danger, and the thought that she would only have learned about it through the grapevine if circumstances hadn't thrown them together this last time was nearly intolerable. "Would you have told me you'd enlisted? If you hadn't run into me?" she asked.

He frowned, his gaze fixed on a point just past her ear. "I didn't see any reason to. I didn't think it would matter to you one way or the other. Also, I was afraid you might take it the wrong way."

"What way is that?"

He brought his gaze back to her, his handsome face troubled. His fair hair, still damp from the rain, hung in tatters over his furrowed brow, and his eyes were blood-shot. When he smiled at last, it was almost heartbreaking. "I didn't want you to see it as some ploy to get you to marry me."

Elizabeth's heart swelled with the knowledge that he still loved her, and at the same time it distressed her to think of the misery it must cause him. "And all this time, I thought you were angry with me."

"I was. Fit to be tied, as a matter of fact." His smile faded. "If that bum had been around, I'd have punched his lights out." He meant AJ, of course. AJ, who was miles from here, perhaps never to return. She felt something twist in her gut but quickly pushed the thought from her mind. Right now this was about Bob, and he deserved bet-ter than to be treated like some poor substitute. "I did everything I could to forget you," he went on. "I went out and got drunk every night for a week. I even tried dating other women." The sheepish look on his face told her how well that experiment had gone. "Nothing worked. The trouble is, Bets, you're it for me. You'll always be my girl."

Her mouth twisted in a mirthless smile. "It would be better if you hated me. Why do you have to be such a nice guy?"

He shrugged. "I can't help it. Guess I'm just built that way."

"You're not making it any easier, you know."

"Maybe I don't want to make it any easier." He reached across the table and took her hand. "The thing is, Bets, I've been giving it a lot of thought. We were together a long time. I guess it's only natural to wonder if the grass is greener on the other side when you're looking to spend the rest of your life with someone. I'm not going to lie to you and say I'm okay with what happened. But in a way, I . . . I kind of understand. I'm sick about it, yeah, but I don't blame you. I just hope that once you've gotten this out of your system, you'll see that there are other things in life that matter more than whatever you think you have with this guy."

She started to shiver again. "What are you saying, Bob?"

"I'm saying I still want to marry you, if you'll have me." He brought the tip of his forefinger to her lips, blocking any words of protest before they could form. "No. Don't answer. You'll have plenty of time to think it over while I'm away. Just promise you'll write to me."

"Of course." It seemed the least she could do.

"Promise?" His eyes searched her face. She gave a solemn nod, drawing an invisible X over her chest, and some of the tightness went out of his jaw. "Okay. Good. Because I don't think I could stand it otherwise. Just no 'Dear John' letter, please. If the answer is no, I'd rather you tell me in person."

Elizabeth didn't know what to say. It would have been less cruel, she knew, to give him her answer now than to lend him false hope, but she felt confused all of a sudden, not sure of what she wanted. Maybe because she was still reeling from her grandmother's death, or maybe because she'd realized, sitting here in his grandparents' kitchen, how much she'd missed Bob's companionship. AJ's vague assurances and the few cursory lines on the postcards he'd sent seemed all at once puny weighed against the goodness and security of the life Bob was offering.

"Just come back, that's the main thing. Don't try to play the hero while you're over there." Whatever her decision would ultimately be, she couldn't bear the thought of a world without Bob.

He drove her home as soon as her clothes were dry enough to put back on. The storm had passed, the only evidence of it now the wet pavement, slick in the glare of his headlights, to which yellow leaves were stuck, like so many telegrams announcing the imminent arrival of autumn.

It wasn't until he pulled up in front of her house that she felt herself grow cold again. She imagined her mother pacing back and forth inside, bemoaning this latest assault on her stronghold, which had turned out to be as flimsy as the straw house in the story of the three little pigs. Still blaming her, no doubt. Elizabeth, having had a chance to think it over, believed she had a better understanding of why her mother had become so unhinged. The fact that Mildred and her mother had never been close had only made it worse: With Grandma Judith's passing, gone, too, was their chance of ever reconciling. But none of that changed how hard it would be to walk through that door. Elizabeth felt sick with apprehension and knew with a sudden, terrifying certainty that if Bob were to ask her to run away with him this very night, she would do so, if only to escape.

He walked her to the door, where they hugged good-bye. Bob's arms around her were a safe bulwark against the storm to come, and she clung to him for a long moment, reluctant to let go. When at last they drew apart, she saw that there were tears in his eyes. She felt a little choked up herself.

"Write to me!" he called back as he jogged down the path.

She smiled and waved to him, but her heart was breaking.

CHAPTER NINE

"I wonder what happened to those letters," Sarah said.

Emily glanced about the darkened living room at the emptied cabinets and sealed cartons as if expecting the letters to magically appear. "They must have gotten lost at some point, maybe during one of the moves." This was the only one of their parents' homes that Sarah and Emily had known, but in the years before they were born, during the time their dad had been in the military, their parents had changed addresses several times.

One thing was for certain: After an entire week of emptying out every cupboard and drawer and sorting through every box of stored mementos, Sarah was convinced that if those letters were still in existence, they would have surfaced by now. Unless . . .

"Dad might've kept the ones she sent him," she said. For all she knew, they could be tucked in his old footlocker, which they had yet to go through—they'd feared that the sight of his old uniform and medals would prove too much for them.

"If he had any letters, I'm sure they're long gone by now," Emily said.

The sisters exchanged a knowing smile. Their father had been the polar opposite of their mother in that regard: He'd seldom saved anything that he didn't absolutely need. Even the workshop where he'd spent hours tinkering with various projects had been as spare and organized as the man himself.

Sarah wasn't one for hanging on to things, either. Besides, what would the letters have told her that she didn't already know? "What's important is that they kept in touch," she said. "I suppose it's true what they say: Absence makes the heart grow fonder."

"Wouldn't the same be true of AJ?"

"Maybe, but she would've needed more to go on than a few postcards. He certainly kept her guessing."

"Men." Emily heaved an exaggerated sigh, flopping back against the couch cushions. "Just when you think you have them where you want them, they up and disappear on you. *That* they're good at."

Sarah thought of her own husband, waiting up for her at their house. Jeff had been a constant in her life since college. He'd been at her side during every one of those painful tests and procedures during the early years of their marriage, when they'd been so desperate to conceive. Just as he had been when she'd finally given birth to their first son and, three years after that, their second. No, he would never walk out on her, any more than their dad would have walked out on their mom.

"Not all men are like that," she said. "Dad certainly wasn't." She didn't point to Jeff as an example, not wanting to rub it in that her marriage was a success, whereas Emily's had failed.

"True," Emily acknowledged. "He was about as loyal and dependable as they come."

"Remember that story Mom used to tell about how he insisted on being in the delivery room when I was born? No one did that kind of thing back then. He had to threaten to sue the hospital before they'd agree to it." Sarah chuckled at the thought of their dad asserting himself. Those who hadn't known him very well had often been fooled by his laid-back temperament into thinking he could be counted on to bow unquestioningly to authority. But nothing was further from the truth, as anyone who'd ever butted heads with Bob Marshall had learned. When he cared deeply about something or saw an injustice, he was always the first to speak out. "A good thing, too, because Mom claimed she wouldn't have been able to get through it without him, it was such an ordeal."

"I guess that's why you're such a goody-two-shoes," teased Emily. "You've been trying to make up for it ever since."

"Speak for yourself. I'm not the one who spilled orange juice all over Mom bringing her breakfast in bed."

"I was eight!" Emily giggled at the memory. "Anyway, Mom told me she'd been looking for an excuse to get rid of that old bedspread for years."

"I just wish she'd told us the whole story." Sarah looked down at the diary she was holding, marking their place with her thumb. They'd read all but the last two entries. "We could have talked about it. Then there wouldn't have been any question."

"About Dad, you mean?"

Sarah nodded, hastening to add, "Not that she didn't love him—we already know she did. I mean, okay, maybe there weren't a lot of fireworks, but what they had was a lot more meaningful than a night of passion under the stars with a man who couldn't give her what Dad could."

"Too bad she couldn't have it all." Emily gazed thoughtfully into the fireplace, where the ashes had long since grown cold.

"Very few people get to have it all," Sarah pointed out, thinking once more of herself and Jeff. As devoted as they were to each other, their lovemaking, she had to admit, had grown a bit predictable with the onset of middle age. At times she missed the spontaneity of their newlywed years.

"If I ever get married again, I'm not going to settle." Emily spoke with a vehemence born of painful experience. "Next time it's going to be the whole package or nothing at all."

"If everyone felt that way, there'd be far fewer babies in the world. Legitimate ones at least," joked Sarah, though she didn't discount the sentiment. She thought Emily was right.

Emily turned to her, frowning. "How do we know she wouldn't have been happier with AJ?"

Sarah sighed. "That's a question I don't think even Mom could answer." Such things fell under the heading of what-if. "We don't even know whether it was AJ who dumped her or the other way around."

"There's only one way to find out." Emily pried the diary from her sister's hands and began to read aloud.

CHAPTER TEN

Dear Diary,

Nothing lasts forever, and I guess that goes for being gossiped about. There are still those who can't look me in the eye without blushing, or scowling, at the thought of my sinful deeds, but most people appear to have moved on. Luckily for me, there's a never-ending supply of fresh scandals in this town, so I'm quickly becoming old news. Now that Bob and I are communicating again, if only by mail, I'm even back in my mother's good graces—tentatively, that is.

I suppose I should be content with that, but there's a hole in me that no amount of buried hatchets or letters from Fort Riley can fill. I can't stop thinking about AJ, wondering where he is and if he's thinking of me, too. I still get postcards from time to time, which tell me more about what's new with him than what's in his heart. Never more than a few lines that anyone, including my mother, could read (which I have no doubt she does) without getting any big ideas. I haven't given up on him entirely. But that sense of certainty I once had is gone. I don't know what the future holds for AJ and me. How can I pin my hopes on a man who hasn't even told me he loves me? Who doesn't even have a forwarding address? Bob, on the other hand, is fully prepared to marry me even though I cheated on him. If that isn't love, I don't know what is.

∽

Indian summer had passed into autumn. The leaves falling from the trees were a match for Elizabeth's mood: It felt as if she were gradually drifting back to earth after her ordeal. The shock of her grandmother's death had given way to acceptance. And a new scandal in town had the gossipmongers buzzing—Sarah Hutchinson, a girl she'd gone to school with, had shocked everyone by running off with a married man—so Elizabeth was no longer on the hot seat. However, life as she'd known it would never be the same again.

For one thing, she now knew who her true allies were. Not the fair-weather friends who used to invite her to parties but people like old Mrs. McCracken down at the drygoods store, who during her ordeal had confided that she waited on certain customers—meaning those who'd made rude comments about Elizabeth—only out of financial necessity; otherwise she'd have told them to take a hike. And several members of her former congregation had expressed outrage at Reverend Freimuth's making an example of her and told her how much they missed seeing her on Sundays. Amelia Whitman, a friend of her mother's whom Elizabeth had known since childhood, had reportedly gone so far as to vigorously defend her to a bunch of the biddies on her church committee.

There was Mr. Arno, too, who'd shown his true colors in her darkest hour. In him, she'd found a father figure, however grumpy at times, to whom she could go for advice or help in solving a problem. He was even giving her extra hours, in addition to a small raise, to aid her efforts to save money for her own place.

Ingrid had come around eventually, holding out an olive branch in the form of the bridesmaid gown Elizabeth had relinquished some weeks before. They'd made peace, and at Ingrid's insistence, Elizabeth had agreed to resume her place in the wedding party. At the same time, Elizabeth knew that a basic trust had been broken on both sides that would never be whole again, however much they might pretend otherwise. She could only hope that they'd forge a new bond one day as wives and mothers. In the meantime, they were on friendly terms, though spending far less time together than in the past.

Elizabeth spent her free time taking long walks or going on drives through the countryside in the used Pontiac sedan she'd purchased with some of her savings. The fresh air and solitude helped clear her head and put things into perspective. She still thought a lot about AJ, but no longer to the exclusion of all else. Lately it was Bob who'd been on her mind more and more.

He wrote to her at least once a week from Fort Riley: light, newsy letters filled with amusing stories about his adventures at boot camp. It was obvious, reading between the lines, that he was well-liked by his fellow recruits, which didn't surprise her. In school, Bob had been one of the more popular boys and often the object of hero worship. Elizabeth didn't doubt there were men in his squad at

Fort Riley who looked up to him in the same way, and she could easily imagine him playing big brother to the ones who were homesick or struggling to keep up. It made her worry a bit less, knowing he would have buddies to watch his back in combat.

For her birthday, Bob had sent her a box of fancy stationery, a gentle reminder that didn't set too serious a tone.

She wrote back faithfully, as promised. In her letters, she kept him abreast of the latest goings-on: the raise she'd been given at work and the new church she'd joined; the flood at the hat factory that had been quickly contained before it could cause any serious damage; the stray puppy that had turned up on their doorstep, which the Simmses next door had taken in, Mildred being allergic to dogs. She wrote, too, about the films she saw and the books she read. "I'm halfway through *From Here to Eternity*," she'd informed him in her last letter. "Besides being highly entertaining, I think it paints a pretty accurate picture of what it was like during the war. If you're not sick to death of the military by now, I think you'd enjoy it. I'll send you my copy when I'm done with it." Bob had written back that he didn't have much time for reading these days but to send it anyway; he was sure he'd enjoy it when he got around to it. In the meantime, care packages from home were always greatly appreciated, he hinted broadly, especially baked goods.

The postcards she received from AJ, in contrast, were few and far between and always seemed to have been dashed off in a hurry. The most recent one was from Galveston, Texas, where he'd found work in the oil fields. It was only a temporary gig, he'd written, until he could see about another opportunity he had cooking on the back burner. He was hoping to see her soon but couldn't say when he'd be back in town. The only indication that he and Elizabeth were anything more than friends was the one line scrawled at the bottom of every postcard: "Miss you."

Elizabeth told herself he was being circumspect because of her mother, who wasn't above steaming open a letter or listening in on a call. And while that notion was certainly valid—even the limited contact with AJ was a continuing source of friction between her and Mildred—with each passing week that brought little or no word from AJ, it was getting harder to convince herself that he loved her enough to come back for her.

It was hard not to compare him to Bob, who not only faithfully corresponded with her but was responsible for the thaw in the atmosphere at home. If AJ's postcards were delivered into Elizabeth's hands in tight-lipped silence, Bob's letters were always presented with a smile and a pleasant remark and provided her and her mother with one of the few topics of conversation on which they were on safe ground.

One night at dinner, her mother inquired, "Will Bob be coming home for Christmas?"

"I don't think they give leave to soldiers headed overseas," Elizabeth told her. Bob had completed his basic training but was still marking time at Fort Riley, awaiting deployment.

Mildred paused in the midst of sawing at her roast beef to bestow one of her rare smiles upon Elizabeth. "Well, then, if that can't be arranged, you could always pay him a visit. I'm sure he'd welcome it."

"Mother, I—"

"Christmas would be the perfect time to announce an engagement, don't you think?"

Elizabeth eyed her mother in dismay, but Mildred appeared utterly guileless for once, as though it were a perfectly normal observation—as though they were talking about whether it might snow on Christmas or whether the carolers would be making the rounds this year. Mildred seemed to take it for granted that sooner or later, she'd come to her senses and marry Bob.

"That would mean a summer wedding," Mildred went on. She skewered a cube of roast beef with her fork and popped it into her mouth, chewing thoughtfully. "We'll have to pick a date soon, though. Those slots get booked months in advance. And there's so much to do before then."

Elizabeth put her fork down. "Mother, what gives you the idea there's even going to *be* a wedding?" Even if she were to accept Bob's proposal, which was far from guaranteed, she would insist that they elope. After what she'd just been through, she couldn't face an elaborate wedding orchestrated by her mother.

"Of course there's going to be a wedding," Mildred replied in the same tone with which she might have asked Elizabeth to pass the salt and pepper. But Elizabeth caught the glint of steel behind her pleasant expression. "Bob's been big enough to forgive you. Not every girl in your shoes would be so lucky. And I can't think of a single one who'd be foolish enough to turn down such an offer."

The subject, as far as Mildred was concerned, was closed.

But when the holiday season finally rolled around, it brought an entirely different sort of surprise. On Christmas Eve, Elizabeth was leaving work with plans to head downtown for some last-minute shopping before the stores closed when she noticed the solitary figure of a man on the sidewalk below the front entrance. It was snowing, and from where she stood on the steps under the building's shadowed portico, she couldn't quite make out his face. He appeared to be waiting for someone, which was odd—the only one left on the premises besides her was the night watchman. Mr. Arno, in a show of holiday spirit, had decided to close early, so all the other employees had gone home hours ago. The only reason she was still there was because she'd had some last-minute paperwork to clear off her desk.

She began descending the steps, and the man started toward her, pausing under a streetlamp as he approached. As he stood caught in the pale cone of light, in which a swarm of snowflakes darted and spun as if alive, his face turned up to her and his blue eyes blazing amid all that whiteness, Elizabeth let out a small gasp of recognition.

AJ.

He was leaner than before, as though stripped down to the bare essentials, the cleanly hewn planes of his face even more sharply defined. He wore a sheepskin jacket with its fleece collar turned up and cowboy boots that had stamped a path in the crisscrossing tracks left by passersby on the snowy sidewalk. He wasn't wearing a hat, and she noted that his hair was shorter than it had been when she'd last seen him. It made him appear older somehow, though no more settled.

He slowed as he drew near, as if uncertain what his reception would be. Elizabeth was uncertain as well. How was she supposed to react after all this time with almost no word from him?

When he reached her, the corners of his mouth lifted in an easy smile that sent her heart aloft.

"Hey, lady, need a lift?"

"I have my own ride, thank you very much." Elizabeth wasn't going to give him the satisfaction of thinking she'd been pining for him all this time.

"Did you get my postcards?" he asked.

"I did. I would've written back if I'd had a forwarding address." There was a note of reproach in her voice.

"I was never in one place long enough," he explained. "But I came back, didn't I? Just like I said I would."

"And you thought I'd just be sitting on the shelf, waiting to be dusted off?"

"So you're mad at me now, is that it?" AJ didn't seem perturbed by her display of temper.

She stared at a snowflake stuck to one of his eyelashes, resisting the urge to brush it off. Airily she replied, "Mad? Why should I be mad? Really, AJ, it's not like I don't have better things to do than sit around waiting to hear from you." The words sailed forth on a frosty plume of breath.

Her hands were stinging from the cold, and she realized that, in her excitement at seeing him, she'd neglected to put on her gloves. Hastily she fished them from her coat pocket and tugged them over her numb fingers. When she looked up again, he was regarding her with bemusement.

"Can we go somewhere?" His affectionately teasing tone gave way to a more serious one. "Just to talk," he added at the sharp look she flashed him. "I can see there are some things I need to clear up."

"All right," she said with a show of reluctance. "But don't think I can be bought off with some flimsy excuse."

They decided against going to the Rainbow. Half the town congregated there, and it was especially crowded this time of year—they were sure to be spotted by someone they knew. The Brass Rail was equally out of the question. So they ended up driving all the way out to Cross Corners, on roads made nearly impassable in spots by the bad weather, to the tavern where AJ had taken her on a summer evening, a lifetime ago, when the night had been alive with fireflies instead of falling snow and she'd first learned that not every good thing in life came neatly wrapped.

The mood there was far different tonight. Other than a handful of die-hard patrons, the place was empty. Most of the locals appeared to be at home celebrating the holiday with their families. The upright piano against the wall by the door sat shrouded, the old Negro piano player nowhere in sight. The only music was that of the jukebox, at present Tony Bennett crooning his latest hit single, "Because of You," to the off-key accompaniment of a grizzled veteran at the bar.

"Thank God it's not a Christmas carol. It'd drive away even old Saint Nick," remarked AJ with a laugh, glancing at the would-be tunesmith, who was clearly soused to the gills, as they settled at a table in back with their drinks—whiskey and soda for him, gin and tonic for her.

Reminded of what day it was, she said, "I can't stay long. My mother's expecting me." Mildred was having some of the neighbors over for a little holiday supper, and Elizabeth had promised to help.

"So why don't you phone her and tell her something came up?" He gestured toward the pay phone in back, then fished a dime from his pocket and plunked it down on the table in front of her, saying with a grin, "It's on me. That way you have no excuse not to let me buy you dinner."

Elizabeth felt the gulf between them widen further. Bob would have understood, without her having to explain, the impossibility of attempting to palm off her mother with an excuse. Did AJ even have a clue of what she'd been through these past months, mostly on account of him?

But if she was angry, it didn't alter the fact that she was glad to see him. All the old feelings had been stirred up, and only pride kept her from expressing what was in her heart. Suppose his feelings toward her had changed? Was that what he'd come to tell her? "I can't," she told him, not without regret. "She's having some people over. It's a holiday tradition—she does it every year on Christmas Eve. Anyway, I promised to help out, and I don't want to let her down." AJ didn't respond. He just sat there smiling at her as if he knew it was only a matter of time before he wore her down, which nettled her. "What? You don't believe in tradition?"

"Sure I do," he said, raising his glass to his lips. "It's just that I don't have much experience in that department."

"Your grandparents didn't celebrate holidays?"

"Not so's you'd notice. If I needed new underwear, my grandmother would wait until the middle of December to buy me some, then wrap it up and put it under the tree. The only time I ever got a toy was in school. One year I got this little tin wind-up car, but my grandfather confiscated it when I brought it home. He told me our family didn't accept charity. That," he said, "was Christmas in our household." He spoke without a trace of self-pity, as though merely reporting the facts, but Elizabeth felt a tug of sympathy nonetheless. At the same time, it highlighted the stark differences in their upbringing. Mildred, despite her faults, always went out of her way to make the holidays festive. She never stinted on material things, either.

"What are your plans for tomorrow?" Elizabeth inquired lightly. She wasn't expecting a gift but hoped he'd want to spend at least part of the day with her. That is, if he wasn't planning to take off again.

"Don't know yet. I'm sort of playing it by ear."

In other words, his plans didn't include her. Elizabeth felt a tender spot in her chest bloom into an ache. Why had he bothered to come back at all? Clearly it wasn't to see her. "So what is it you wanted to tell me?" she asked somewhat brusquely. The Tony Bennett song had given way to Nat "King" Cole crooning about chestnuts roasting on an open fire. At the bar, the tin-eared drunk sat slumped over his bottle of beer, while the bartender was busy tacking up a string of Christmas lights that had come loose in one spot.

AJ leaned forward, growing suddenly animated. "What do you know about computers?"

"Not much," she replied, puzzled by his question. What did computers have to do with anything? "I know they exist, that's about it."

"Just wait. One of these days they'll be so much a part of our daily lives, we'll wonder how we ever did without them," he said excitedly. His eyes glittered in the dim light, and flags of color stood out on his cheeks. "Ever heard of a semiconductor? They're what drives a computer. Well, there's this fellow I know out in California who's gearing up to produce them on a mass scale. He's been getting together the financing, and it looks like he's finally ready to pull the trigger. That's where I come in. You see, he's offered me a job. The pay isn't much to start with, but it's a once-in-a-lifetime opportunity to get a foothold in something that's going to be big—I mean really big." He paused to knock back a gulp of his drink, the rattling of the ice in his glass making her think of dice in a game of chance. The enterprise he was describing sounded just as risky. "Of course it would mean we'd have to move to California," he went on in the same fevered tone. "But I've already looked into it, and there are plenty of places for rent. Eventually we'll be able to buy our own house. Out there they're springing up faster than cornstalks."

He was almost stumbling over his words in his enthusiasm. But Elizabeth was still stuck on a single, defining word. "'We'?" she echoed in numb disbelief.

"You and me." AJ seized her hands. "That's what I wanted to tell you. I would've told you sooner, but I wanted to have a real offer in hand before I did. Don't you see? I couldn't come to you with a bunch of pipe dreams." He tightened his grip on her hands, never taking his eyes off her face, as if he could make her understand through the force of his gaze alone. "I guess I'm not doing a very good job of it," he said, "but what I'm trying to say is . . . Elizabeth Harvey, will you marry me?"

For Elizabeth, time stood still and the earth stopped turning. There was only the rushing of blood in her ears and the single thought pealing inside her head like a church bell: *He wants to marry me.* It filled her the way water fills an empty jug, spilling over when it reached the top. When she could no longer contain it, she put her head down on their joined hands and began to weep.

She wasn't just weeping out of joy and relief. She was weeping for Bob, too. Dear Bob, who would soon be off fighting in Korea, the only thing keeping him going the thought of being able to return to her one day. She hadn't led him on, but the mere fact that she was corresponding with him implied some kind of commitment. Also, she'd vowed to spare him a 'Dear John' letter, and if she were to accept AJ's proposal, it would mean breaking that vow.

Marrying AJ would also mean giving up the only life she'd ever known. It wouldn't be the worst thing in the world if her mother were to banish her; in some ways, it would be a relief. But did she want to leave behind the entire community? Like it or not, she inhabited this town the way she inhabited her body: It was part of her. Yes, there were those in Emory too small-minded to see past their own noses, but most of the people were generous and good-hearted. There were few in Emory who wouldn't give the shirt off their back to help someone in need. It was par for the course when a farmer fell ill or became injured for his friends and neighbors to pitch in, working extra hours to sow his fields or bring in his crop. Driving by the Findlays' farm not long ago, she'd seen a new barn going up, a swarm of people, most of them volunteers from the look of it, knocking themselves out to get it raised before the cold weather set in.

This was where her father and his people were buried. And where she'd hoped to raise a family of her own one day. If she were to move to California, whom would she know other than AJ?

She raised her head, using the heel of her hand to brush the tears from her cheeks. "I'm sorry," she said, reaching for her napkin, which she used to dab at her eyes. "I don't know what came over me."

AJ looked a bit befuddled, but he attempted to make light of it by teasing, "Hey, I know I'm no catch, but a guy doesn't expect a woman to burst into tears when he proposes to her."

"It's not you. It's just . . . it's a little overwhelming is all."

"I guess I kind of sprang it on you, didn't I?" he acknowledged sheepishly.

"You could have given me some warning."

"In that case, I'll warn you that I'm not about to take no for an answer."

"Let me at least sleep on it." In her present state, she wasn't capable of deciding which way to go down a one-way street.

He regarded her intently for a moment before giving a slow nod. It wasn't the answer he'd been hoping for, but he was trying to put the best face on it. "Fair enough. Just tell me one thing."

"What?"

"Do you love me? Because damnit, woman, even if you don't, I love you enough for the two of us."

A bolt of lightning shot straight down through the pit of her stomach. Love? It was the one thing she hadn't taken into account. The one thing she couldn't measure against all the rest. She could no more hang a future on it than she could on air. At the same time, she knew it was that very air upon which her existence depended.

She looked him straight in the eye when she said it: "I love you. God help me, I do."

His smile was slow to break but dazzling when it did. "I'm going to hold you to that."

Tomorrow she would have to make the most important decision of her life. But tonight she wanted to savor this moment and the giddy sense of possibility it brought.

By the time they'd finished their drinks and stepped outside, the snow had stopped falling and a hush lay over the white-blanketed landscape. It was as if the world had taken a collective breath. Colored lights twinkled on the houses across the street, reflecting off the snow piled against doorways and under eaves. The sky overhead was so clear and sharp that the stars seemed newly minted, just for them.

"Merry Christmas," he murmured, taking her in his arms.

They kissed, standing there in the snow under the stars. AJ's lips were soft against hers, asking rather than demanding, his gentle embrace leaving room for the unspoken question between them. They stayed that way even after they'd stopped kissing, their arms around each other, Elizabeth's head resting on AJ's shoulder. From inside drifted the sound of the jukebox, Mario Lanza singing "Be My Love" in his soaring tenor. Spontaneously they began to sway in time to the music, both thinking the same thing: Christmas had come early this year.

He stroked her hair, whispering in her ear, "I love you, Elizabeth Harvey. Whatever happens, don't ever forget that."

"I won't." She smiled into his shoulder, a secret smile just for her.

Whatever happened, she would always remember this Christmas. For the rest of her days, she would hold it as close to her heart as she was holding AJ right now. It would be the still breath at the center of each thought, the rest note between each beat of life's song. Someday, when she had children, she would wish the same for them: a moment in time when love was that all mattered.

CHAPTER ELEVEN

Sarah and Emily were wiping their eyes as they turned the last page of the diary. Emily said in a choked voice, "So that's it? We don't get to find out how it ends?"

"We know how it ends," Sarah said. "She picked Dad."

Emily should have felt comforted by that fact—as Sarah had pointed out earlier, they wouldn't have been here otherwise—but she felt a strange melancholy nonetheless. "Poor AJ. He must have been devastated."

"I don't doubt it."

"Mom, too. They were obviously crazy about each other."

Sarah cleared her throat, speaking briskly in an effort to keep her warring emotions in check. "Even so, she must have thought Dad was a better bet." Naturally she wasn't sorry their mother had chosen their father over AJ. What troubled her was that it had been such a heartbreaking choice.

Emily was similarly torn. Yes, she was the daughter of
Bob and Bets Marshall, but she was also a romantic. Her
own marriage had failed because she'd married for the
wrong reasons. What would have happened if she'd waited
for the right man instead of settling for the first one to
come along? If her mother had taken a chance on AJ instead of opting to marry her father?

She unfolded herself from the sofa, where she'd sat nestled beside Sarah, stretching her long limbs to release the
kinks. "It could have had something to do with the war."
She wandered over to the fireplace, where half-a-dozen
framed photos were still displayed on the mantel, ones she
and her sister had yet to divvy up. She picked up an old
black-and-white photo of their father in his army uniform,
gazing at it with new eyes. "What if she'd sent that 'Dear
John' letter and he'd gotten killed? She would have felt
partly to blame. Knowing her, she wouldn't have been able
to live with herself."

"You make it sound like she only married him out of a
sense of responsibility."

Emily turned to find her sister frowning. "I'm sure that
wasn't the only reason," she said. "He made her happy. And
didn't she always tell us that being happy was the most important thing in life?"

Sarah, feeling suddenly restless, got up and carried the
empty jelly jars and wine bottle into the kitchen. A few
minutes later, Emily came padding in after her. She looked
as lost as a prodigal daughter returning home after an absence of many years to find her family gone and her house

occupied by strangers. In one hand was the diary and in the other what looked like an ashtray.

Emily handed Sarah the ashtray. "I found it under the china cabinet. It must've fallen out when we were emptying the cupboards."

Sarah eyed it curiously—as far as she knew, neither of their parents had ever smoked—before deciding it must be a relic from a previous era when it had been considered polite to offer cigarettes to guests. Another reminder of the mysterious life their parents had shared before she and her sister had come along. She was about to toss it, then thought better of it and wrapped it in newspaper, tucking it into the carton with the glassware. Throughout the packing process, she'd been ruthless, but now she couldn't bear the thought of tossing away even this small, worthless item. Tonight the house and everything in it seemed steeped in significance.

She straightened to find her sister standing by the breakfast nook, staring sightlessly out the window into the dark, the diary clutched to her breast. She looked so much like their mother that it gave Sarah a start. "I wonder if he ever got over it," Emily said softly.

"AJ? I'm sure he did eventually," said the more practical-minded Sarah. "He probably married and had kids of his own."

"Do you think they kept in touch?"

Sarah shook her head. "If there'd been any letters from AJ, we'd have found them by now."

"Maybe she didn't keep them. After all, she didn't save the ones Dad wrote her."

"Well, it was a difficult time. I'm sure she didn't want to be reminded of it."

Sarah finished tidying up the kitchen, throwing out the Chinese takeout containers, running the garbage disposal, and sponging off the counters. The day after tomorrow, the new owners, a young couple, would be taking possession of the house, but for her this would always be home—the home her mother had taken such pride in. She knew Bets would have wanted it left in order.

When Sarah looked up again, her sister was still staring out the window. "I wonder if he's even still alive," Emily said.

Sarah squeezed the sponge dry and placed it on the counter by the sink. "How would we even track him down to find out? We don't know anything about him except that he had a rough childhood and that his uncle was a son of a bitch."

"We could try calling Information. Maybe he's listed in the phone book."

"We don't even know his last name."

"Good point." Emily fell silent. "I wonder why the entries stopped after that Christmas," she said after a bit.

"For one thing, Mom and Dad got married right after that," Sarah reminded her. Their parents had eloped before the year was out. "And what if Dad had stumbled across the diary by accident? It would have been hurtful for him to find out that she still had feelings for AJ."

"Not that he would have let on," observed Emily.

Their father hadn't been one to wear his heart on his sleeve. Their mother had blamed it on the war. Whatever the reason, he hadn't been forthcoming either in emotional displays or in talking about the past. Yet there had been no stinting in the affection he'd lavished on his two daughters. He'd known how to have fun, too, despite his serious side. Sarah recalled how he had entertained them every night before bed when they were little, doing magic tricks or strumming on the ukulele. Every summer they would go camping by the lake, and he'd tell stories by the campfire—not tales of his childhood but fantastical made-up adventures—and do goofy things like turn cartwheels on the beach, making them shriek in delighted embarrassment. After church on Sundays, while their mother fixed breakfast, he would read aloud to Sarah and Emily from the Sunday comics—*Dick Tracy, Gasoline Alley, Dagwood and Blondie*—giving voices to the characters and acting out their parts while the two girls sat on his lap, transfixed.

That reminded Sarah . . .

"Speaking of Dad, we have to decide what to do with his ashes."

They had been debating the matter all week while packing up the contents of the house. Emily thought the ashes ought to be scattered on the lake where they'd gone camping every summer. Sarah was in favor of keeping them in the rosewood urn their mother had had specially made to house them; she'd volunteered to take custody of it. They hadn't discussed what to do when their mother's time came; it was too much to contemplate on top of struggling to cope with the day-to-day reality of watching her slip away bit by bit. The one thing they agreed on was that her remains should also be cremated. They were sure that was what she would have wanted.

Emily turned around to face her sister. "There's no rush, is there? We don't have to decide right away."

"What are we waiting for?"

"You know," Emily hinted darkly.

Sarah said it for her. "You mean we should wait until Mom goes."

Emily winced at hearing what they both dreaded spoken aloud. "The doctor said it could be any day." There was fear in her voice but also resolution: She wanted to be prepared when the time came.

"I know, but I'm not ready," Sarah said in a small voice. Usually she was the strong, sensible one, the one everyone else leaned on, but she didn't feel very strong at the moment. Wasn't it their mother who'd always said the tree that didn't bend was the first to break in a storm?

"I don't think we'll ever be," said Emily mournfully.

Sarah set aside her apprehension for the time being. "Let's talk about it tomorrow, shall we? I won't be able to think straight until after I've had a night's rest." She and Emily finished taping up the last of the cartons; then Sarah reached for her coat, draped over the back of a kitchen chair.

"See you in the morning?" Emily said, picking up her own coat.

Sarah nodded. "Ten-thirty. I'll meet you there."

It had become their ritual to meet at the nursing home every Sunday morning after church. The rest of the week was catch-as-catch-can, with Emily and Sarah taking turns visiting their mother and Sarah's husband and sons occasionally tagging along. But Sundays were for the sisters alone, a time when they drew support from each other and discussed what needed to be done.

"What do you think we should do with this?" Emily retrieved the diary from the kitchen table, where she'd placed it while putting on her coat. It was the last item from the house that hadn't been packed, thrown out, earmarked for Goodwill, or set aside for sentimental reasons.

Sarah was about to suggest that Emily take it home with her and tuck it away in a safe place, but then she had a better idea. "Bring it with you tomorrow when we visit Mom. She should have it."

Emily looked dubious. "I don't know. She's pretty out of it."

"Still."

Emily tucked it into her shoulder bag. "You're right. It's what she would have wanted."

Outside, Sarah hugged her sister good-bye before they headed off to their respective cars. "I'm glad we found the diary—or it found us," said Emily in parting. "It's weird to think of Mom with another man, but at least she got to experience true passion in her lifetime, even if it wasn't with Dad. How many of us have that?" It made it a little easier letting go of her, knowing she'd had those memories at least.

❧

The Miriam Hastings McDonald extended care facility didn't advertise itself as such. There were no signs out front, and casual passersby might take the gracious old brick building with its impeccably kept grounds for a private school, or perhaps a church retreat. As Emily pulled into the circular drive, she noticed that the dahlias in the center island, going to seed just two days before, had been replaced by rows of hostas and sweet william. Here, death wasn't a cause for mourning. Whenever a resident passed, a memorial was printed "in celebration of" that person's life. Unlike other extended care facilities, where such events were downplayed or swept under the rug, MHM even held a memorial tea for those who wished to pay their respects. The staff encouraged the residents to think of one another as family and the families to feel connected to the painful and sometimes long-drawn-out process of letting go of a loved one.

The more sentient and able-bodied residents lived in the main house, with its antique furniture, well-stocked library, and daily ritual of afternoon tea. Those whose minds were gone or who were bedridden occupied a separate wing, reached via a pair of double doors secured by a keypad and wide enough to accommodate a gurney. Beyond those doors, the setting was purely institutional. Each of the rooms in the B wing held a hospital bed and various outlets to accommodate monitoring and life-support machines, should the need arise. The nurses, licensed RNs as opposed to the LVNs who made up the majority of the staff in the main house, wore blue scrubs and were trained in life-saving techniques. Those machines and techniques were seldom put to use, however: The majority of the residents at MHM had living wills stating that no extraordinary measures should be taken.

Elizabeth Marshall was no exception to the general rule. In the wills she and her husband had had drawn up years before either had become ill, they had made it clear that neither wished to survive the other for any longer than was humanly sustainable. In fact, they'd often expressed to each other, privately so as not to upset the girls, the wish that they not be separated at all. Their preference would have been to go together, like the old couple who'd gone down with the *Titanic* rather than be parted in death.

But life took its own course. At the age of seventy-nine, Elizabeth's husband of more than fifty years had been diagnosed with cancer and was gone within six months. Their daughters were surprised by how well she appeared to cope with his loss. Even so, Sarah and Emily began imploring her to sell her house and move into something smaller and more manageable, closer to where they lived so they could keep an eye on her. After weeks of such entreaties, Elizabeth took both of her daughters to lunch and, over iced tea and Cobb salads, set them straight. "I don't want you girls to think that just because Dad is gone, I need looking after," she told them in the same firm tone she'd used when they had tried to push the limits as children. "You have your own lives. I'll manage just fine on my own." What she didn't tell them was the reason she was coping so well: She knew it wouldn't be long before she'd join their father.

There was nothing wrong with her at the time aside from the general aches and pains of old age, but she had a strong and not entirely unwelcome premonition of her own death. She didn't believe in ghosts, nor was she given to superstition. Nonetheless, she kept smelling her husband's aftershave wherever she went, not just on the clothes he'd worn. She was aware of his presence in other ways as well, as she went about the daily business of reorganizing her life on a smaller scale, as keenly as if he were sitting across from her at the table when she took her solitary meals, or lying beside her in bed at night. So palpable was his presence at times that she reached out to touch him, and it came as a mild shock to have her fingers meet with nothing but air.

Not being one to leave for others what she was perfectly capable of doing herself, Elizabeth proceeded to put her affairs in order. She cleared the closets of all her husband's things, donating his suits to Goodwill and giving away the more personal items to her daughters and grandsons—his watch, his wedding ring, his leather briefcase, the trophy he'd won in an amateur golf tournament—keeping only a handful of photos and mementos for herself, along with the rosewood urn that housed his ashes. She hired a handyman to take care of the long list of house repairs she'd put off while her husband had been ill and, last but not least, had her lawyer draw up a trust placing everything she owned in her daughters' names.

Even so, it came as a shock to Sarah and Emily when, a little more than a year after their father's death, their mother was felled by a massive stroke. The doctors were able to detect some brain activity, but because she was unable to speak, or even move, they couldn't say how much or how little she was aware of what was going on around her. Tests were still being done to gauge the full extent of the damage. In the meantime, their mother remained locked inside her frozen body, the woman who had been Elizabeth Marshall suspended somewhere in the recesses of her damaged brain like an embryo in its mother's womb. She was capable of thought but not of communicating it. She recognized her daughters when they came to visit, but they no longer recognized her.

Had she been able to communicate, she would have told them not to shed any tears for her: Death was a welcome alternative to life without their father. She would have told them, too, not to mourn her after she was gone. She would have reminded them of the oft-told story of the day, before they were born, when she and their father had taken the train to visit a colleague of his, and they'd accidentally been separated. He'd gotten off at one of the stops to make a phone call, an important one having to do with the reason for their trip, which had so preoccupied him that he hadn't noticed the train pulling out of the station. By the time he'd caught up to it, hours later, Elizabeth had been so relieved to see him that she'd taken him in her arms without a word of recrimination. But she'd never forgotten the panic she'd felt as the train left the station and she realized he wasn't on it. She wanted her daughters to see their father's death as if he had just stepped off the train before her. Soon she'd be rejoining him.

Emily was the first to arrive on the morning after she and her sister had finished packing up the house. Sarah showed up a few minutes later. On their way to their mother's room, they stopped briefly to chat with their favorite nurse, a Mexican woman named Marta who was around their age. They often remarked that it would have been nice to have known her in some other capacity—say, through a book club or fund-raising committee. They were grateful that Marta always treated their mother with dignity and spoke to her as though she were capable of comprehending. They appreciated such gestures because they alleviated some of the guilt they felt at not being able to care for Elizabeth themselves.

"She's asleep at the moment," Marta informed them. Her normally animated face was grave. "I'm glad you're here, though. I think this would be a good time for you to say whatever you need to say to her. I know it seems like she can't hear you, but I have a feeling she does. I'm sure it'd be a comfort to her." They understood what she was really saying: that it wouldn't be long now.

They could see it for themselves as they stood in the doorway to their mother's room, speaking in hushed voices so as not to wake her.

"Does she look any worse to you?" Emily asked.

Sarah shook her head. "Hard to say." There was so little left of their mother. She was so frail that it seemed as if any but the gentlest touch would cause her bones to snap. The skin stretched over her shrunken frame was nearly transparent, and her silver hair, once so abundant, was wispy as a toddler's.

Sarah found herself thinking of a former neighbor who'd lost a child. For months afterward the grieving mother had refused to wipe clean the sliding glass doors to her patio, which had borne her little girl's handprints. To Sarah, her mother seemed as insubstantial as those ghostly handprints. Still, the thought of losing even this last vestige was unbearable. The only thing that provided any comfort was the knowledge that Elizabeth would be joining their father. However much Bets might once have loved another, she'd been devoted to her husband to the end.

"You know what I did when I got home last night?" Sarah leaned into the door frame, her eyes on the still, slumbering form on the bed, so corpselike she would have grown alarmed if not for the monitoring devices quietly beeping overhead. "Jeff and I stayed up past midnight looking at baby pictures of our kids." She turned to give her sister a small, wistful smile. "It goes so quickly, doesn't it? I remember when *we* were little. It seems like just yesterday."

"I once asked Mom why there were hardly any pictures of Dad in our photo album," recalled Emily, wiping a tear from her eye. "She reminded me that he'd been the one *taking* the pictures." She managed a wobbly smile. "They were such a team. It's hard to imagine there was ever a time when they weren't."

"I think it was the tough times that brought them closer." Sarah thought of how much closer she and Jeff were as a result of all they'd been through. Even the battles had made their marriage stronger in the end.

"Which reminds me . . . " Emily withdrew the diary from her purse. "I was looking at it again last night after I got home. I even had a dream about it." She gazed down at it, rubbing a thumb over its worn maroon cover. "In the dream, Mom was her old self again. She hugged me and told me everything was just as it should be." Emily swallowed hard, fighting back tears. "Do you think Marta was right, that she understands what's going on? Or is that just wishful thinking?"

"I like to think she understands," said Sarah, struggling against tears of her own.

As if in answer to their question, their mother's eyes fluttered open. But if the sisters had hoped for a miracle, there was none to be found. Sarah experienced the same shock she always did at the sight of those blank, cloudy eyes staring into nothingness. That was the hardest part for her: seeing the spark in those eyes that had once defined their mother extinguished.

"Still, I wonder if she'd want to be reminded," Emily said, looking down at the diary in her hands. "Maybe that's why she never told us about AJ."

"Or maybe it was because she wanted to set a good example," Sarah speculated. "How would it have looked to us if we'd known our dad wasn't her first choice? What kind of message would it have sent? That you should marry for security instead of love? That fulfilling your duty is more important than following your heart? Where would we be now if we'd been taught that?"

"I might've married someone else," offered Emily glumly.

"And I might not have married Jeff." Before Sarah had met her husband, she'd had a boyfriend named Dennis Rowe who, if she'd had a checklist of qualities she was looking for in a mate, would have fulfilled every one. What if she'd married Dennis even though she hadn't been mad for him?

Quietly the sisters entered the room. Emily placed the diary on the bedside table next to the vase of yellow roses Sarah had brought from her garden on her last visit. The roses were nearly spent, and a few of the petals broke off at the brush of her hand, scattering over the diary's frayed cover. Emily started to brush them away but thought better of it. The petals seemed to represent the small death that had taken place in those pages penned in their mother's girlish hand. The death of a love, a life, that might have been had she made the choice to take a different direction.

Recalling Marta's words, she turned her anguished gaze to the shrunken figure on the bed, who bore only a vague resemblance to the once vibrant Elizabeth. She placed a hand on her mother's forehead, gently stroking her hair. "Mom? It's me, Emily. I don't know if you can hear me, but . . . " She faltered a bit before forging on resolutely, "I . . . we . . . " She cast a teary-eyed glance at her sister. " . . . want you to know that everything really *is* okay. We're doing fine. Not as fine as if you were with us, but we're managing. Just in case you were worrying."

Sarah sank into the chair beside the bed, dabbing at her eyes with a tissue. "What Emily's trying to say, Mom, is that if you need to be with Dad, we understand. You have our blessing."

Sarah leaned to kiss her mother's cheek, laying a gentle hand over Elizabeth's gnarled ones, folded over each other as if in final repose. Their mother's countenance was peaceful. If the sisters hadn't known better, they might have imagined that the wisp of a smile on her lips was meant for them.

❧

The following evening brought the news they'd been dreading. Emily, when she got word, immediately drove over to Sarah's house, where the sisters consoled each other while Sarah's husband made pancakes for supper—the only thing he knew how to cook. Sarah's two teenaged boys, seventeen-year-old Curtis and fourteen-year-old Elliot, respectfully refrained from texting their friends or playing computer games. Yet without those distractions, they seemed at a loss, as if not knowing what to do with themselves. They had adored their grandmother, but to them death was an alien concept. This was the second time they had experienced it in their immediate family, and they didn't quite know what was expected of them.

Elizabeth's remains were cremated two days later, and the memorial service took place the Sunday after that. She'd been active in the community, and numerous friends and acquaintances of all ages turned out for the service. Hundreds of people poured into the church, many of whom had an anecdote to share afterward at the reception at Sarah's house.

Elizabeth's hair stylist tearfully told Emily about the time just after he'd found out he was HIV-positive, when many of his regulars had begun defecting to other stylists at the salon. When Elizabeth had learned of it, she'd made a point of coming in more often than usual, scheduling appointments with him for the middle of the day, when the salon was at its busiest. Eventually some of the other ladies, seeing that she wasn't afraid of infection, had come around.

An attractive middle-aged woman from the book club their mother had belonged to told Sarah of how vigorously Elizabeth had campaigned in favor of the classics, titles some of the other women in the club had feared would be too heavy. "I never would have read *Anna Karenina* if it hadn't been for your mother," she said, dabbing at her eyes. "And to think what I would have missed!"

The elderly owner of a mom-and-pop grocery store in their old neighborhood spoke fondly to the sisters about how their mother would often stop by just to chat in the lonely days after his wife had passed away. Once, he said, she'd brought him a bag of grapefruits from a neighbor's tree. When reminded that he had a plentiful supply of grapefruits in his store, she'd replied, "Yes, but these are sweeter."

Olive Diefenbaker, a dear old friend of their mother's, told the story of how Elizabeth, when asked each year what she wanted for her birthday, would suggest something outrageously unattainable: an iron that wouldn't leave scorch marks, a dryer that didn't eat socks, cut flowers that wouldn't wilt. Once Elizabeth had confided to Olive that she had always secretly coveted the green dress with a plaid lining that Ann Miller had worn in *On the Town*. After years of this, Olive had finally thrown up her hands, declaring, "You're impossible! If you won't tell me, how am I supposed to know what to give you?" Elizabeth had responded with a smile, "Olive, dear, I thought you already knew. All I want is your friendship, and you've already given me that."

Sarah's modest frame house was so packed that people were spilling out onto the patio despite the fact that it was a bit chilly outdoors. It was late in the afternoon before the crowd began to disperse. Sarah and Emily were clearing away the dirty plates and platters of leftover food when they came across a last stray mourner. An older gentleman, whom they'd noticed only peripherally before, was now seated on the living room sofa, quietly gazing out the window as if lost in thought. He hadn't offered his condolences at the church, so they'd pegged him as a casual acquaintance who'd merely come to pay his respects.

He rose with some difficulty as they approached. The sisters could see that he must have been quite handsome in his youth. He still was, in a craggy, all-American sort of way, like an older, thinner version of Robert Young in *Marcus Welby, M.D.*, with his twinkling blue eyes, full head of silver hair, and broad shoulders from which his conservative black suit hung as if from a sturdy wooden hanger. He moved slowly, as if even the simple act of taking a few steps were an effort, and they noticed he favored his right leg. They also noticed a slight tremor in his hand as he extended it to them.

"Bob Miller," he introduced himself, engulfing first Sarah's, then Emily's hand in his firm, dry grip. He seemed familiar to them for some reason, though they were certain they'd never met him before. "Pleasure to meet you. I'm an old friend from Emory. I was so sorry to hear about your mother." In his deep rumble of a voice, they heard genuine sorrow rather than mere sympathy.

"Thank you for coming," Emily murmured politely. She felt more than a bit numb from the hours of holding it together, from the warm pressure of hands and lips that had been besieging her all day.

"It was a long trip," he said, "but I wanted to pay my respects."

"You came all the way from Nebraska?" Sarah struggled to make small talk. She felt as drained as her sister, but years of keeping up with small children, and now teenagers running in and out of the house all day, had left her better prepared to withstand the strain of this day that seemed as if it would never end.

Bob Miller smiled, showing a mouthful of teeth too even and white to be his own. "You bet," he said, and they heard the unmistakable gee-whiz cadence of the Midwest in his voice. "Believe it or not, I still live in Emory, though it's a lot more built up now. Raised a family there—three boys and a girl. After my wife died, my son Pete—he lives in Kearney—asked me to move in with him, but I told him no. I was born in Emory, and I reckon I'll die there."

"Funny, I don't recall my mother ever mentioning you." Emily was frowning slightly, as if trying to place him.

He blinked, seeming a bit taken aback, but was quick to recover. "No, I don't suppose she would have," he said regretfully. "It was a long time ago, and we didn't exactly part on the best of terms."

Emily and Sarah exchanged a glance.

"Why don't you have a seat?" offered Sarah. "I'll bet you could use a cup of coffee. I know I sure could."

The two sisters went to fetch coffee and refreshments, returning a short while later to find Bob Miller standing by the fireplace, holding a framed photo from the mantel— the one of their parents on their wedding day. In it, their mother was dressed not in white but in a pale-pink suit with a fitted skirt and peplum jacket, and a smart little hat with a veil that came down over one eye. Their father looked uncharacteristically sober-sided in a suit and tie. They'd decided against a church wedding, or so the story went, because they'd been in too big a hurry to get married.

"She was so beautiful, your mother." The old man gazed at the photo a little while longer before returning it to its spot on the mantel. When he turned to face them, his eyes were bright with unshed tears, and he wore an odd, wistful smile. "I loved her very much at one time, you know."

Emily and Sarah exchanged another look, both wondering the same thing: Was there yet another surprise in store when it came to their mother's love life? Or was this man merely referring to a long-ago crush? "Were you and my mother close?" Emily probed discreetly, placing the tray she was carrying on the coffee table before sinking down next to her sister on the sofa.

"Oh, yes, quite close." The old man fell silent for a moment, his expression pensive, then shook himself free of his reverie and slowly lowered himself into the easy chair opposite the sofa, gripping its arms to brace himself. "I'll tell you the story if you have the time," he said once he was comfortably settled. He directed his keen, blue-eyed gaze at the sisters. "But first, there's something I should ask. What did your folks tell you about how they fell in love?"

Sarah poured the coffee and handed him a cup. "I don't know that there was a particular moment when they fell in love. I think it was just something that grew over time. After all, they'd known each other since childhood." She saw no reason for this man to be told their mother's entire history.

Emily wasn't so circumspect. "They didn't talk much about those days," she explained, "but we came across Mom's old diary when we were cleaning out her attic, so we were able to piece together some of the story. We know she was involved with someone else before our parents were married. Someone named AJ."

Bob stared at them, looking perplexed for some reason. "AJ was your father," he said.

This time the glance that Emily and Sarah exchanged was a knowing one. It was obvious to them now that the old man was missing a few of his marbles. "I'm afraid you're mistaken." Sarah addressed him as gently as she did old Mr. Maynard next door, the senile World War II veteran who stood outside his house every day in full uniform, saluting passersby. "Our father's name was Bob. Bob Marshall. You must have known him if you all went to school together."

"Sure, I knew him."

"Well, then, you must have gotten him mixed up with—" Sarah started to say. Before she could finish, she was jolted into silence by the old man's next words.

"AJ was just what he called himself back then."

Now Emily and Sarah thought it was they who must be going mad. "I don't understand." Emily was slow to react, her thought processes dulled by grief and the day's outpouring of sympathy. "Mom wrote in her diary about someone named Bob. We just assumed it was our dad."

"That would've been me." The old man went on to explain, "You see, there were three boys named Bobby in our class. I was one—they called me Bobby M. Then there was Bobby Newland . . . and your dad. Needless to say, our teachers were always getting us mixed up." He chuckled at the memory. "Used to drive your dad crazy because I got to be 'Bobby M.' while he was just plain old 'Bobby.' But it wasn't until after his folks were killed in that car wreck that he took on the nickname of 'AJ.' A for Adam—that was his father's name—and J for Jeanette, his mom's."

Sarah and Emily had known that their father had been raised by his grandparents, but they had never met them— their great-grandfather had died before Sarah was born, and their great-grandmother, who'd suffered from dementia, had been confined to a nursing home for years. Now it dawned on them that their great-uncle Cole, of whom they'd only heard occasional mention (their father had always discouraged any suggestion that they invite him to visit by saying he and Cole didn't see eye to eye), was the brutish uncle their mother had referred to in her diary, whose car AJ—their dad—had torched in a fit of temper. And that it had been their *father* who'd done time in juvenile detention. Their heads were reeling with the revelation; it was too much to take in all at once. How could two such different men—the elusive, free-spirited AJ and the stable, down-to-earth Bob Marshall—be one and the same?

And what about the nickname "AJ"? As the mists began to clear, Sarah recalled that their mother, in moments of affection, would occasionally call their father "Jay." Sarah had taken it as a reference to an old family joke—their mother used to tease that he must have been a blue jay in another life because of the chattering of power tools forever drifting up from his basement workshop. But now it took on new meaning. If this past week hadn't been such a blur, she might have thought of it sooner.

"When did he go back to being Bob?" she wanted to know.

"In the service," replied the old man. "Whatever name they called out during roll call, that was what you answered to. I ought to know; I was there. We were in the same company. We fought together in Korea."

"Wow." Emily could see now why she'd confused the two men in the diary. They'd *both* served in Korea.

"Your dad was drafted shortly after I enlisted, just after he and your mom eloped," Bob Miller went on to explain. "I don't mind telling you it was a bad day when he got assigned to my company. We were just getting ready to ship out. I remember thinking that the big guy upstairs must be testing me—not only was I going to get shot at over there, I'd have to rub elbows with the man who'd walked off with my girl." He smiled ruefully as he spoke, as if at the youthful passions of someone he used to know, saying in a gentler tone, "But while we were overseas, I got to know another side of him. He was a good man, your dad. The plain fact is, I owe him my life."

The sisters sat riveted, staring at the old man as if he'd pulled a rabbit out of a hat, heedless of the hoots and hollers coming from the next room, where Sarah's teenaged sons were engaged in a spirited game on their Wii, and the clattering from the kitchen as Jeff cleaned up. Was there no end to the twists and turns of this bizarre tale?

"Oh, I know what you're thinking," Bob Miller went on. "I had every right to hate his guts, and I won't deny that I did. But we were soldiers first, so we had to set aside all that other stuff. Easy to do once we started seeing combat. Over there, all I could think about was staying alive. Your dad ever tell you about the Battle of Hill Eerie?" They shook their heads, and he continued in his rumbling baritone, "It was in March of '52. Orders came down that we were to take the outpost, so they set up a couple of patrol squads around the perimeter and sent in twenty-six of us from the 3rd Platoon—me and your dad, we were in the rifle squad. That, I can tell you, was the longest night of my life. And we were still at it come morning. The Chinese had us outnumbered and were gaining ground. The command post had radioed that reinforcements were on the way, but from where we sat, it didn't look like they'd make it in time. At one point, we were pinned down by machine-gun fire. Four of our men were killed, several more wounded. I caught a bullet in my leg." He slapped his right thigh. "It was your dad who held them off until the reinforcements arrived. So, yes, I owe him. I wouldn't be alive to tell the tale if it weren't for him."

Emily and Sarah knew their father had earned an medal for bravery in battle, but the details had been vague until now. What wasn't a surprise was that he'd risked his own neck to save others. On or off the battle-field, he'd never been one to take a passive role. Like the time back in the 1960s, before the passage of the Civil Rights Act, when a few racist members of their home-owners' association had tried to keep a black family from moving into the neighborhood. He'd gone door to door, gathering signatures on a petition, as a result of which the Greens had been able to buy the house next door to theirs. Over the years, the two families had become close friends. In fact, Vernon Green had been among those to give a eu-logy at their father's funeral. Both Ethel and Vernon, along with their grown children, had attended Elizabeth's funeral as well.

"I lost touch with him after the war," Bob said with some regret. "He and your mom had moved to California. I stayed in Emory, as you know—that's where I met my wife. Later I heard your dad was working at some com-puter company. To be honest, I never thought it'd amount to anything. Back then we all thought that was pretty high-tech stuff. I couldn't foresee a day when there'd be a com-puter on every desk." He smiled and shook his head. "Funny how things work out."

"Mom wrote in her diary that he used to make a living doing caricatures at county fairs," Emily said. "Do you know anything about that?"

Bob Miller took a sip of his coffee, the tremor in his hand causing the cup to rattle in its saucer before he raised it to his lips. "Sure, I remember. He was pretty good at it, too, from what I heard."

"I wonder why he never said anything to us." Emily glanced at Sarah, frowning.

"Oh, he never thought much of that," Bob said. "A cheap parlor trick was what he called it. I imagine he figured that if the people he worked with knew about it, they wouldn't take him seriously."

Sarah turned to Emily. "Remember those little cartoons Dad used to draw on napkins to keep us entertained in restaurants? And the posters?" She brought her gaze back to their guest, explaining, "Every year he'd design the poster for the community center's Christmas fair. People couldn't get over how professional-looking they were, but my sister and I just took it for granted that everyone's father could draw that well." She realized now that their father must have channeled most of his creative energy into his job as head of R&D at Hewitt, where he'd been in charge of implementing new ideas that required complex designs.

Emily nodded slowly. She was remembering things, too. Like how her parents had been a closed corporation in some respects. They'd loved her and her sister, of course, but their focus had always been on each other. She recalled the looks they would exchange across the dinner table, as though sharing some private joke. And the way their mom would drop whatever she was doing when their father arrived home from work each night and run to meet his car as it pulled into the garage. She thought of the jewelry box her father had made Elizabeth for Christmas one year, the hours he must have spent in his basement shop fashioning all its little drawers, sanding and varnishing it, and how her mother had treasured that box more than any of the jewels it contained.

He'd been the love of her life. How could Emily have doubted that for a second?

"Did Mom ever send you that 'Dear John' letter?" she asked.

Bob Miller's face creased once more in a rueful smile. "No, as a matter of fact, she didn't. She kept her word. She came to see me instead—rode the bus all the way down to Fort Riley to tell me in person. It was a gutsy thing for her to do. I knew that even then, though I'm afraid I didn't take it so well at the time. I didn't think I'd ever get over it, but eventually I did. In the end, she did me a favor. Otherwise I never would have met Maggie." His eyes misted over at the mention of his dead wife. "I wish your mother could've known my Maggie. She'd have liked her."

They chatted a while longer over coffee and cake. Sarah invited him to stay for supper, and Emily offered to put him up at her place for the night. Bob thanked them warmly but declined both invitations. He was scheduled to fly home that evening, he told them, and had arranged for a car to take him to the airport. When the car arrived, the sisters were sorry to see him go. They understood why their mother had been so fond of him. They also understood why she'd chosen their father. Bob Miller was a nice man, but he wasn't a patch on their dad.

"Can you believe it?" declared Emily as they shut the door behind him. "Imagine if he hadn't shown up. We'd have spent the rest of our lives wondering if Mom married the wrong guy!"

"Which, as it turns out, wasn't the case," Sarah said with some relief.

"What if it wasn't a coincidence, his showing up like that?" Emily said as they gathered up coffee cups and crumb-littered plates. She paused to direct her gaze at her sister. "What if it was all part of some cosmic plan? I mean, do you really think our finding the diary was an accident? Because I'm not so sure it was." Her more practical-minded sister might scoff at the idea, but she believed there were things that were beyond their ken.

Her sister wasn't scoffing, though. Sarah's expression was serious, even thoughtful, as she considered the possibility that fate had played a hand in their discoveries. At last she exhaled deeply and said, "Who knows? Maybe it is some sort of divine plan. The important thing is, we know what to do now."

"About what?"

"I think we need to take a trip—to Emory."

Emily picked up at once on her train of thought. "Does this have something to do with Mom's and Dad's ashes?"

As soon as Sarah described what she had in mind, Emily realized it made perfect sense. In fact, she wondered why she hadn't thought of it herself. The only thing that came as a surprise was that it had been her sister—sensible, down-to-earth Sarah—who'd come up with such a wonderfully grand and romantic scheme.

⁓

The town of Emory wasn't at all what they'd expected when they arrived late in the day on Saturday of the following week. They'd pictured a sleepy little burg with a main drag made up of local eateries and mom-and-pop shops. Instead, as a result of the spur that had connected it to I-80 in the early '70s, the former backwater was now a thriving community. The only part that still matched their parents' description was the surrounding countryside, which was mostly cornfields stretching as far as the eye could see. Housing developments had encroached in the areas just outside town, and there were other signs of "progress" in the form of strip malls and a brand-new sports arena, but for the most part, the farmlands were intact. If the bulk of them had been swallowed up by large agribusiness growers, there were still quite a few small farmers, many of whom were carrying on the traditions of their parents and, in some cases, their grandparents.

One of those farmers was Quentin Findlay, who, along with his wife, Priscilla, and their two sons, Grant and Jerod, farmed the land that had been passed down to him by his folks. When the phone call came from a woman identifying herself as the daughter of Bob and Bets Marshall, Quent was somewhat taken aback by her request. He recalled the name, though. He'd been a young boy when the original barn behind his house had burned down, but he remembered it as if it were yesterday—the awful sight of the barn in flames, the night sky so brightly lit it might have been day. All these years later, it came as a mild shock to hear from the daughter of the man briefly suspected of setting that fire.

"Dad felt real bad about it afterward," Quent told her over the phone. "He never meant to accuse the boy. He just thought it was something the police ought to look into. After that girl—your mother, was it?—come forward to vouch for him, Dad wanted to apologize for what he'd put him through and to thank him for helping rescue the animals, but he'd already left town."

Quent went on to say that Sarah and her sister were welcome to have the run of the property. He insisted, too, that they come for lunch on Sunday. He wouldn't take no for an answer.

The sisters located the Findlay farm easily enough, using the directions Quent had given Sarah over the phone. As they pulled into the tree-lined dirt drive in their rental car, they found it to be just as they'd imagined: a four-square white clapboard house with a deep screened porch, shaded by a majestic old elm. Several dogs lolled in the yard, and chickens roamed freely, pecking at the dirt. Out back stood the red-painted barn that Quent had referred to as the "new" barn, though it looked as weathered as if it had stood there forever. Cows and horses grazed in the adjoining pasture, beyond which lay the endless-seeming cornfields they'd driven past on their way in.

Sarah and Emily were greeted warmly by their hosts, who stepped down off the porch to meet them as they approached along the walk. Quent Findlay was a tall, rangily built man with close-cropped salt-and-pepper hair, his lined face cured by the sun to the color and texture of rawhide. His wife, in contrast, was youthful-looking and rosy-cheeked despite the fact that she and her husband were about the same age. She was a tiny woman, but Quentin teased, "Don't let her size fool you. She can lift her weight in bales of hay and outwork most of the men around here."

She also turned out to be an excellent cook. Emily and Sarah were treated to a feast of roast pork, homemade biscuits, corn on the cob, and a salad made from vegetables from the garden, washed down by gallons of sweet iced tea. For dessert, Priscilla had made a berry cobbler and homemade ice cream. The sisters couldn't remember when they'd last eaten so much in one sitting. It amazed them to watch Quent and Priscilla and their sons, a pair of strapping young men in their late twenties—neither of whom was married, Priscilla reported with an exaggerated rolling of her eyes—have two helpings of everything, as though the huge meal were nothing out of the ordinary. What also amazed the sisters was that there wasn't an ounce of fat on any of them.

"I would if I could get away with it," said Sarah, declining the second helping of cobbler Priscilla offered her. She sighed, patting her belly with its roll of excess flesh. "Maybe I should take up farming. That way I could eat all I want and be as skinny as you."

Everyone laughed, Priscilla grousing good-naturedly, "Skinny? I call it being worn down. After thirty-five years of taking care of this place and looking after these brutes—" She glanced fondly around the table at her husband and sons. "I'm surprised there's anything left of me."

After lunch, while Priscilla was washing up, Quent took Sarah and Emily on a tour of the property. He showed them around the "new" barn, from which they entered the fenced-in pasture, high with grass at this time of year. After they'd walked at least a quarter of a mile, they arrived at a spot where the pasture sloped up to meet a flattened knoll ringed with trees. Beyond that lay the cornfield. "This here's the spot," announced Quent, pointing up at the knoll.

"You're sure of it?" asked Sarah.

"Sure, I'm sure," he said. "My dad took me out here himself the day the police came to investigate."

Emily shivered a little under the warm sun, feeling the past encroach on the present.

Sarah felt it, too. She had to clear her throat, not once but twice, before she could reply, "Thank you. For everything. Not just for your hospitality but for allowing us to—" She broke off, unable to finish the sentence, she was so choked up. She looked down at the rosewood urn she was carrying, which contained her mother's ashes. The matching one was cradled in Emily's arms.

"All right, then. I'll leave you to it," he said somewhat brusquely, sounding a bit choked up himself, as if the occasion were stirring up memories of his own.

As soon they were alone, Sarah turned to Emily, giving her a long, meaningful look. The time had come for them to see this through.

They hiked to the top of the knoll, where they stood looking out at the grassy, sun-struck pasture rolling away on one side and the cornfield, with its rows of head-high stalks, on the other. From this distance, the barn and farm-house below looked exactly as they must have in their parents' day.

"It feels like we're in church," said Emily, speaking in a hushed voice. The silence was broken only by the hum of insects and the distant lowing of cattle. "Do you think we should say a few words?"

"It doesn't have to be formal," said Sarah. "Just say what's in your heart."

Emily squeezed her eyes shut and tried to summon words worthy of the occasion. But the only ones that came to mind were, "Mom, Dad, I wish you were here. I miss you." A tear leaked from under one closed eyelid.

"They are here, in a way." Sarah spoke softly. "Can't you feel it?"

Emily concentrated hard, but all she could feel was the sun on her face and the fly tickling her arm. After a moment, she opened her eyes to fix her sister with a mournful gaze. "It's weird, but in one sense, I feel like I've only just gotten to know them. All these years, I never thought of them as being anything other than our parents. But they had lives of their own apart from us. They were passionate. They took risks. How could we not have known that about them?"

"I think all children feel that way about their parents," observed Sarah as she gazed out at the fertile land of their ancestors. "We don't want them to be like the rest of us. Otherwise we'd have to see them as fallible, and think how scary that would be." She thought of her own two boys and how she had sought to protect them when they were young, to keep them from finding out how scared she'd felt at times, how utterly ill-equipped to mold these two living, breathing lumps of clay committed to her care. If she possessed an extra measure of strength today, it had come from repeatedly patching over those areas of weakness.

"I suppose you're right," said Emily. "But it would've been nice to have known Elizabeth and AJ."

"Maybe that's why Mom kept the diary. She knew we'd come across it one day."

Emily saw them juxtaposed in her mind—Bob and Bets, AJ and Elizabeth—like overlapping images in a double-exposed photo. Now that she had the missing pieces of the puzzle, it all made sense. She had a better idea of why her parents had been less than forthcoming in sharing their history. Elizabeth wouldn't have wanted to be reminded of her fraught relationship with her mother or the turbulent episode leading up to her decision to marry "AJ." For her father, it hadn't been just the war. He'd had a hard life before then: the tragic deaths of his parents, his life with cold and unloving grandparents, the uncle who'd physically abused him. No doubt he'd wanted to shield his daughters from that ugliness. So he'd created the impression of an ordinary childhood—not unlike Bob Miller's—in much the way she imagined he'd once sketched his caricatures: a line here, a suggestion there. He'd poured everything else into his family, to whom he'd given all he had to give: his heart and soul, his tender, loving care, his undying devotion.

With a certainty just as deep and true, she knew this was what he'd have wanted. For him and his beloved wife to be joined in death, in this place, as they had been in life: two halves of the same whole.

"Shall we?" Sarah interrupted her sister's reverie.

Emily looked at her and gave a solemn nod.

Each, in turn, pried open her urn.

The wind had picked up, and it snatched at the handfuls of ashes before they could be tossed, scattering them into the air. The finer ashes gathered into funneling clouds that rode the currents, dipping and swaying with each new gust, skimming over the rustling green corridors of corn before swooping up high to kiss the treetops. Almost as though they were dancing.